The Curse Of The Zombie Zoo

Erik Masterson

ISBN: 1-4783-5616-2
ISBN-13: 9781478356165

Dedication

To my dad, David, thanks for listening and always being there.

Prologue

A long time ago, the year was 1986 or thereabout if you must know, in a quiet town called Forest Heights in the Ozark Mountains of Arkansas, when things were different than they are now, an adventure began. Adventures tend to happen by accident, which is the best way possible really. One ends and one begins, always. Otherwise it would be quite a boring place we live in. And nobody likes being bored. So, let's get on with it! This is what happened all those years ago when Philip, Sam, and Abby Pruitt, so young and so brave, had a really big adventure.

Part I

1

Philip watched the two figures walking along Crooked Creek, a girl holding a red and white peppermint swirl umbrella and a boy wrapped in a green poncho, quickly closing in on his hideout.

"How do they always find me?" Philip wondered. "They know I'm fishing." Philip took his baseball cap off and wiped his forehead. He liked being out by himself. Just him and the fish...even on a day like today after a promising bright morning became dreary and wet thanks to a stray stubborn rain shower.

Abby stopped when she found footprints collecting rain in the sandbar along the creek. She knew her older brother was close. She glanced around and spotted him standing under a gray bluff on the other side of the creek. She waved. Philip watched as his brother and sister ran toward his hiding place determined to pester him. Sam found a place to cross the water, leaving Abby to find her own way.

Perfect boulders poked out of the water ready to be jumped on. The rain made the rocks slick but Sam nimbly hopped across to the middle of the creek.

"Just one more leap, and I'll be across," Sam thought as water rushed in front of him. With a great leap he landed with a mighty splash a good three feet from the far bank. Sam's head disappeared beneath the water. Flailing every which way, the rapids dragging him downstream, he reached out and grabbed a gnarled root sticking out from the bank.

Sam heard Philip laughing at him as he struggled out of the water through the tangled mess of roots and mud. Philip almost slipped down the bank from laughing so hard.

"I don't need your help," Sam yelled as he grabbed hold of the sturdy bamboo that grew thick along the creek. Scrambling through the dense undergrowth, his green poncho was now useless shreds. He stood there, covered in mud and wet leaves, his sandy hair dripping wet, with a huge grin smeared across his clever face.

"You're a ham, Sam," Philip said.

"No. You are!" Sam fired back as he yanked his tattered poncho off. He stood there examining his wet shorts and T-shirt.

Still laughing, Philip asked, "Where did Abby go?" They looked back across the creek to the empty sandbar.

They searched upstream, following the bluff and watching the creek for signs of their sister. Ahead, an old oak tree, its roots undercut by the creek long ago, lay across the water creating a sort of bridge. They saw Abby studying the fallen giant about to do something impulsive.

Abby was pretty smart for eleven. Everyone knew it. She liked to figure out what to do on her own and generally she did this in a reasonable, well thought out way, but this time she made her brothers nervous.

Philip and Sam watched, helpless, as she closed her umbrella, tucked it into her belt strap, and climbed up through the tangled mess of dead branches spanning the creek. Everywhere she stepped the branches creaked and cracked under her slight weight. After a few unsure minutes, she climbed out onto the barrel-like tree trunk above the creek.

Halfway across the tree, Abby looked upstream. The rain had turned to a pesky drizzle, but the sky now looked dark and ominous. She crouched down to balance herself and stared at the approaching black clouds. Then something caught her eye far up the creek. What she saw thrilled her. She loved animals: fur or no fur, big or small, cute or smelly. It didn't matter to Abby.

"Can't be," she thought, staring hard, afraid to blink and lose sight of what can't possibly be. At a bend in the creek, she saw what looked like a zebra standing lonely on a gravel bar. She brushed aside her dark hair that constantly fell across her face to get a better look. "White stripes, check; black stripes, check; totally cute, check," she thought quickly to herself.

"No way!" she shouted. Her mind raced.

The little zebra, wobbling on its thin legs, appeared confused as it headed upstream toward some unknown destination. The animal stopped, turned back, and seemed to look right at Abby. She felt her heart stop. Even from this distance, she saw dark dirty stains on its black and white coat.

"It's scared and hungry. I have to do something," Abby thought. The sky continued to grow darker by the second, and then ferocious gusts of wind threatened to knock her off the toppled tree. The creek was rising rapidly from the gully washer of rain from those dark clouds up the valley and she didn't have a minute to spare.

Philip startled her out of the rescue fantasy forming in her head.

"Get off that tree and get over here!" he yelled. He and Sam anxiously waved at her to hurry. This made Abby feel stubborn. More stubborn than usual.

"I know what I'm doing!" she yelled. "Stupid boys. They can't tell me what to do!" she thought.

Abby kept watching the zebra as it started walking toward her. Suddenly the dark menacing clouds thundered into the creek valley and a wall of rain engulfed the little zebra.

"Oh, no!" Abby cried.

As the torrent of rain advanced toward her, Philip and Sam frantically yelled at her to move. She stayed crouched on the tree, dazed and frozen in place, until her brother's voices broke her trance.

Abby scrambled like a giant spider monkey across the last of the tree trunk and leapt into the thick bamboo along the bank.

Her brothers lost sight of her for a minute as she fought her way through the crowded bamboo. Pulling herself up the creek bank to the shelter under the bluff, she said, "You dummies won't believe what I just saw!"

"What did you see? Sasquatch?" Sam asked.

"Whatever!" she yelled as she stood straight, eye to eye with Sam. She shook her head, flicking her wet hair from her pretty face, to reveal her smart, hazel eyes.

"You're so weird," Sam said.

The three of them took shelter from the torrential downpour under the bluff. There was enough dry wood from abandoned animal nests at the back of the shelter to build a crackling fire.

The downpour turned into a steady, cold rain. After the rain, a heavy fog settled in the creek valley. It felt late for two o'clock in the afternoon. From their shelter under the bluff, they watched the creek rise up and up, ever closer to their hideout. The flood both frightened and exhilarated them. Crooked Creek looked like the Mississippi River. The brown churning water spread like long fingers into the forest on both sides of the creek. Leaves, limbs, and trees surged downstream. They saw the tree Abby had crossed pull free of the bank and wash away downstream.

Abby explained what she saw as she tossed a bamboo leaf she had absentmindedly tied in knots into the fire.

"You're crazy," Sam said. He popped another Boston Baked Bean into his mouth. Philip kept "just in case" stuff in his backpack for just such occasions.

"Look, I'm telling you there is a baby zebra somewhere over there, and we are going to rescue it," she proclaimed pointing across the creek. Not convinced, her brothers sat and listened while munching on snacks.

"I bet it went into the woods to escape the flood." Her voice sounded a bit shrill as she tried to make her case. "Someone has to be missing it!" She said desperately.

"What are we supposed to do? Just skip across this giant flood? Or maybe we could just build a catapult and launch you across." Sam wasn't having any of it.

"I have a better idea. Let's go home," he said.

Philip took a break and walked to the back of the shelter to rummage through the leaves and debris. He found a few dry sticks and tossed them on the fire. Smoke drifted up and found its way out from the bluff edge; embers glowed in the ring of rock encircling the small fire. It smelled good in their cozy hideout. Even the rain soaked land outside smelled good to them.

"Abby, I don't know. I see cows every time I come out here," Philip said moving the glowing coals in the fire around with a stick. He liked to fish on Crooked Creek, but he really hadn't ventured this far upstream before.

"And don't forget those really small cows. I think they call them baby cows," Sam teased.

Abby felt annoyed. Her eyes narrowed into that dangerous squint of hers. Philip knew that look. He sat back down and reached for his backpack. Rummaging around in it he found a bag of Nacho Flavored Corn Nuts—her favorite. He lobbed them over to her.

As she tore into the bag of crunchy, cheesy, goodness, Sam said, "Maybe you just saw a big fat dirty skunk." Before Abby could react and unleash her fury on her brother, they all froze. A sound in the fog silenced them.

2

They crouched on their hands and knees and leaned outside the shelter, staring intently into the fog. They needed to hear that sound again.

The odd, yet familiar, trumpeting resonated again down the foggy valley from far upstream.

Philip broke the silence, "That can't be what it sounded like. Can it?"

"Yes it is and you know it," Abby whispered.

Sam chimed in and ruined the moment. "So what! There's an elephant in the woods. Big deal. Let's go home." Abby and Philip ignored him.

"Have you ever heard that before?" Abby asked Philip.

"No. But I've never gone any further up the creek."

"So?" she asked.

"So, the best fishing spots are down by the low water bridge and it's easier to walk home from there," Philip said. "There's nothing up here for miles except for a few cows. There aren't even any roads that cross the creek upstream as far as I know."

She kept on. "Are you sure?"

"Nope," he answered.

Philip ended the conversation by helping Sam. Sam filled an old glass jug washed up by the creek with water to extinguish the fire. Philip kicked some dirt over the coals. The blackened embers sizzled and smoldered and were finally silent. The wet ash smelled pungent and bitter.

"Now, how do we get out of here?" Sam asked.

Philip knew they couldn't go downstream. The creek followed the bluff all the way to the low water bridge.

"Let's head upstream and see if we can find a better way up," Philip said. "Highway 7 parallels Crooked Creek. All we need to do is find a trail or something and hike up to the highway."

Sam led the charge, followed by Abby and Philip. They passed under a waterfall cascading off the bluff from the rain and followed a narrow trail that skirted the base of the bluff. Animals had cleared the well-trodden path while traveling back and forth from their dens to wherever it is animals like to go.

Ahead, Abby and Philip watched Sam push a dead tree over. It tumbled down the hillside, creating a landside of loose rock. Suddenly, Sam forgot his urge to go home and took off around the end of the next bluff. This was way too much fun for him.

While Abby stopped to tie her shoe, Philip leaned against a tree and patiently waited. He looked down below where the creek left its normal course and flooded the valley. Giant jigsaw blocks of stone lay down there, fallen an eternity ago. Water swirled and eddied around them. He thought it would be fun to come back and explore when the creek was back between its banks.

The peaceful moment ended when they heard a sound like a car falling over a cliff. Along with the screeching metal and shattering glass they heard, "Woohoo!"

Philip ran along the trail, leaving Abby behind. He came to the end of the bluff where he last saw Sam. Philip stopped when he came to the gargantuan pile of garbage. Right off he could tell it wasn't new garbage, it was old. All rust, no plastic. It started below a building at the top of the hill and cascaded to the flooded creek. The garbage of a long gone generation.

Abby ran up next to Philip.

"Wow. Unbelievable!"

They saw Sam standing in the middle of the mass of rusted metal pushing against an old washing machine lodged against a tree. The machine gave way and bounced down the slope, rusty chunks flying off it in all directions.

Throwing his arms in the air, Sam yelled, "Yeeesss!"

Philip and Abby decided to join him in some creative destruction. They broke bottles, kicked at rusty cans, and rolled a few ancient black rubber tires down the slope that splashed and disappeared forever in the flooded creek. They laughed and cheered.

Philip found an old toy truck eaten away by rust. It looked like an old truck he once saw in a black and white movie. He thought if he dug around in the junk he might find some treasures. Once he found a nickel with a buffalo on one side an Indian on the other in the flower bed at the side of their house. He never saw anything like it before.

As Philip imagined finding all sorts of loot, he heard the creak of metal and then a solid slam. He looked up and saw Sam and Abby sitting at the wheel of an old rusty sedan pretending to drive. Spray painted on the driver's side door was the warning: "NOT FOR SALE."

Philip couldn't understand why anyone would want to buy this car, let alone how they could see it down here?

A tree grew out of the car's trunk. The windshield was a spider web of crazed cracks. None of this stopped Sam from pretending to drive down the windiest road ever as Abby adjusted the silent defunct radio while bobbing her head to imaginary music. They were having so much fun that Philip decided to join them.

As he made his way through the rusted mess, he heard a woman's voice shout, "Hey! Who's that down there? You messin' around with my investments!"

Philip saw a woman leaning out from a row of windows that spanned the entire length of the dilapidated building above. White paint peeled away exposing its gray rotting foundation. He didn't know what an investment was but he didn't think they were messing with one.

Sam and Abby couldn't hear the woman yelling at them so they kept pretending to drive. Philip cupped his hands and yelled, "I'm Philip Pruitt. We are trying to find a way out of here. The creek flooded."

"This is my shop; An-Tiques, An-Ticks, An-Junk. I'm Margie Jean!" she proclaimed. "Now you get up here and get those other two out of my husband's car! And make sure they close the doors, too! Don't want the mice to get in."

Margie Jean had a reputation for never forgetting anything—and never throwing anything away. If anyone ever lost anything, they could probably find a replacement in her store. She also had things people didn't think they needed and she would let them know it, too. The name of her place said it all.

After climbing the hill and introducing themselves, Sam and Philip drifted into the large room at the back of the building while Abby chatted with Margie Jean about their escape from the storm.

The storefront, lined with colorful bottles and vases, greeted Highway 7. The old building, dedicated to the past like some Egyptian tomb, felt comfortable and musty. Tables, cluttered with cast off treasures, held hidden bargains. Festive holiday candles stuck up like weeds on every table and shelf, tributes to long forgotten merry holidays. The purpose of everything appeared to be to collect dust. The wooden floors groaned with each step. Forgotten tools, piled high at the back of the store, rusted and waited to be used. Sam flipped through cheesy record albums and eight-track tapes at one of the tables.

"These things could be worth some money in about a thousand years," Sam said.

Philip wandered off on his own as Sam turned to the pile of old farm tools at the back of the shop. He began to feel anxious. It was time to get home and make sense of the days strange events.

Abby and Margie Jean sat on tall stools behind the cashier's counter, sipping tea and eating cookies. Abby listened as Margie Jean rambled on.

"You kids shouldn't have been climbing around in that old junk pile. You could've cut yourselves on a piece of rusty metal and got tetanus. That's bad stuff," Margie Jean said. "And being out in that rain with the chill in the air, you just might come down with pneumonia."

Before Abby could get a word in Margie Jean continued. "I don't know how much longer I can keep this store open. Not as many customers as there used to be. No matter. I have everything I want here and no regrets. I'll probably die behind this counter and someone will find me years later just sitting here stiff as a hog's hide holding my tea cup. No one left to miss me."

"Don't worry, when you get to be as old as I am you won't think I'm so strange," Margie Jean added, laughing.

"I don't think you're that strange," Abby said. "It just sounds like you have been by yourself for a long time. My dad says that when people are cut off from other people they tend to get lonely and lose touch with reality."

"He sounds like a smart fella," Margie Jean said. "I met your father when he was about your age, and I knew your grandpa, Archie Pruitt. He helped me through a very difficult time."

"Really?"

"Yes indeed. It was during WWII. That's when my husband was killed."

Sam came into the front room carrying an old army issue machete and belt, green with brass grommets. He sat next to Philip on a bench. Margie Jean placed her teacup on the counter top and eyed the boys. The atmosphere of the room thickened as she began to tell them all a story they were not expecting to hear.

"It's been nearly half a century since my poor husband passed. That's his sedan down the hill you were sittin' in," Margie Jean said. "Warren and Archie worked together, you know. They were both caretakers at the old Forest Heights Zoological Park."

"At the what?" Abby blurted. Margie Jean noticed Abby's excitement. Philip edged forward in his seat at the mention of the zoo. "There used to be a zoo here? I've never heard that before," Philip said.

"Of course you haven't. Who would want to even mention it? The zoo closing down was the worst thing ever to happen to this town. Very bitter," Margie Jean said. "Now that all the old timers like me are dying off, no one remembers anyway. I bet there are only a handful of us left."

"What happened to your husband, Warren?" Abby said, almost afraid to ask.

"Well, you see, poor Warren and Archie found out that not everything was what it seemed at the zoo. I found Warren in his car down there off the hill, dead at the wheel. He ran that car right off the road. Archie sat next to him unconscious with a bad knock to the head. There weren't any seatbelts back then, you know," Margie Jean explained. "Later, Archie swore he didn't know what happened. The crash knocked the memory out of his head I guess."

"Soon after, the second world war ended and the zoo was shut down completely and no one's been there since," she said.

The story shocked them. Forest Heights had a zoo? Their grandpa worked there? A car wreck, a death, and amnesia? That didn't sound right.

"So where was the zoo?" Philip asked.

"Out in those woods," Margie Jean raised her arm and pointed to the row of windows at the back of the store. They knew where she meant. She pointed toward the woods across Crooked Creek where they heard the elephant trumpet and where Abby had seen the little zebra.

Margie Jean looked thoughtful for a moment. Something in her mind seemed to click into place and an unconscious impulse took hold. Sometimes this is called destiny or fate, other times, a lapse in good judgment.

"Children, I think this would be a good time to give you something." She left the counter and went toward the back of the store. She opened a door that was almost hidden by a wooden cigar store Indian and went inside. They heard furniture being moved around. When she returned, she carried an old brown leather bag.

Margie Jean plunked the crusty thing down on the counter. They gathered in closely around the artifact. It was the size of a gym bag with a double loop handle, a leather strap, and a buckle clasp. The letters "AP" were stitched onto one side. A strong smell of mildew came from the leather.

"This belonged to your grandpa, I think. Never did get to ask him. I just assumed it was his," Margie Jean told them. "I found it tucked into the back of the trunk of Warren's car. The initials are Archie's."

"I want you children to have this. I'm tired of keeping it. It just takes up space. If you don't take it, well, I'm just going to throw it out. Anyway, it was your grandpa's and you should have it." She was determined they take it.

"Can I buy these?" Sam asked, holding up the machete and belt from the before mentioned war. Margie Jean came out of her reverie, back to the present.

"Don't see why not," Margie Jean said. "You've a good eye for old junk, too." Sam paid five bucks for the army green belt and wood handled machete.

"What a bargain," he thought.

Philip went to the counter and grabbed the bag. He was ready to go.

"Thanks for everything, but we have to get home. Sam, Abby, let's go."

"Are you sure?" Margie Jean asked. "It only seems you just got here."

Philip raised his eyebrows at his brother and sister as he was half way out the door. He was feeling antsy.

"Let's go!"

❊ ❊ ❊

3

Sam fastened the stiff army belt around his waist. As they walked along Highway 7 he felt the weapon swinging at his side. He yanked the machete from its sheath with a flourish and held it high, then slashed mightily at an invisible foe, which happened to be the weeds along the road.

"Put that thing up will ya!" Philip yelled. "You're making me nervous." Sam snapped the machete into its sheath.

"We need to talk about all this," Abby said. "We still have plenty of time before we *really* need to be home." They kept walking.

"I have to find out about that zoo. There must be more animals. We have to save them."

Thunder boomed and lightning shot across the once again darkening sky. A big raindrop splashed on Abby's forehead. She looked up, scrunching her face. Another landed in her eye.

"That settles it. I know a shortcut," Philip said. "It's going to keep raining all day." They agreed.

"Great. I'm ready to get home. You do remember its pizza night?" Sam said. They remembered. In fact, nothing was ever too important to make them miss pizza night.

The clouds burst open and heavy rain pelted down. They were quickly soaked as they cut across the steep hill in front of The Church of the Holy Harvest. They felt cold and miserable as they trudged their way up the hill on the squishy rain-flattened grass.

They passed under the imposing cross at the peak of the hill. A sprawling asphalt parking lot encircled the massive church. As they crossed the black, empty lot, they heard an angry voice competing to be heard over the rain.

"Hey! Hey you! I'm talking to you! Don't you know this is private property!" He shouted. He was livid. Outrage and smug holiness radiated from him. Even in the rain, his perfectly manicured gray hair looked like a helmet protecting his head, just as the Lord intended.

"Oh, geez," Philip said under his breath. Sam and Abby turned to Philip.

"That's Pastor Newton. He's got a temper. We gotta get out of here before he has a stroke," Philip said. "Don't look at him. Just keep walking and head toward the trees."

Philip led the way toward the far edge of the blacktop to a thick grove of trees. They walked as fast as they could without breaking into a run, trying to look as inconspicuous as possible, which made them look really suspicious.

Pastor Newton began to yell again, threatening and sanctimonious. "Redemption is at hand! The blood of the cross will wash away your sins and purge all the evils from the world! His eye is upon you! He will not forget your faces! I know who you are!" He was still yelling as they pushed their way into the bushes and disappeared.

A jagged bolt of lightning hit the giant cross at the top of the hill as if Pastor Newton willed it down himself. They heard the deafening roar of thunder that cracked overhead.

They hid under an old cedar tree. Its fragrant branches draped to the ground, protecting them from the storm and prying eyes.

"What was that all about?" Sam asked, catching his breath.

"He's always crazy like that, but he seems to be extra crazy today," Philip replied. "Maybe it's the storm."

"I went to church here with a friend one time and Pastor Newton said some weird stuff. People were talking in crazy voices and babbling, getting up on stage and dancing around. He called it 'speaking in tongues.' I guess people just like that kind of stuff."

"Oh, I don't know," Abby said. "Something's wrong with him. He threatened us when we weren't even doing anything." She was hurt. "What's wrong with this town? I just want to go home." Overloaded from the day's events, she felt disheartened.

"Me, too," Philip said. "There should be a hiking trail in these woods. If we follow it, we'll end up a few streets down from our house. It shouldn't take long."

He pushed his way through the cedar branches, followed by Abby and Sam. They found the trail. It stretched out of sight in several directions, winding its way around trees and boulders. Philip discovered the trail while riding his bike last summer. It was a good place to get away from his brother and sister when he wanted to be alone.

"Wow, this is nice," Sam said, admiring the trail. "And it heads toward our house?"

"Yup," Philip said. "I've ridden my bike through here all the way down to the highway. I've never seen anyone on it, and there's lots of stuff to look at." Philip went left and led them along up the trail.

Walking briskly through the rain, they saw lichen-covered rock walls, a few rock chimney hidden among the trees, and plenty of rusty cans and bottles.

"This looks like an old road," Abby said. "There must have been people living down here a long time ago."

Philip looked back at Abby, who was looking out past the trail.

"There's stuff like this all along here. You're gonna like what's up ahead," he told her.

Soon they heard the sound of rushing water where a narrow path split from the main trail and led to the edge of a steep slope. They looked down into the little valley and at the swollen stream.

In the narrow valley below lay the ruins of a bygone era. There were old walls and broken foundations and plenty of places to explore. A shaft of metal with a giant circular gear stood motionless firmly griped in the rock and rust foundation. Water rushed against the stone foundation.

"What is that?" Abby asked.

"That's an old mill. The water would turn a big wooden wheel that fit with that gear and then it would turn big flat round stones to grind corn and stuff. Sometimes they powered big saw blades for cutting wood," Philip explained it as best he could. "It was a big deal in the old days. Not like today when you can go to the store and get whatever you want."

"Let's go down there," Sam said.

"Later," Philip said. "We're almost home. I promise we'll come back. Plus there isn't anything down there to do except climb on top of the mill," Philip said. He knew the real reason Sam wanted to go down there. "Don't worry. The view isn't that good up there anyway."

Sam gave him a questioning look. "You climbed up there? You're afraid of heights. There's no way you would have climbed up that thing."

"Come on! I'm going home with or without you two dill weeds." Abby stormed off back to the main trail. Philip and Sam followed.

"Wait up! We're coming!" Philip yelled. They caught up with Abby, draping their arms around her shoulders.

"Oh. Abby, you're so cute," they teased her. She acted like she hated it, but they knew she loved the attention. As she squirmed away, she pointed down the trail.

"Isn't that a street?" she asked. Sure enough, it was.

The rain stopped just before they reached their house. The sound of their soggy shoes flip-flapping on the asphalt, and the water squishing in their shoes as they skipped home made them laugh. Abby swung the leather bag back and forth while Philip and Sam made sure to jump in every puddle along the way.

❊ ❊ ❊

4

A concrete driveway led up to big double doors of the basement, which was more like the first floor, of their white two-story house. It used to be a farmhouse surrounded by pasture a long time ago before there was a neighborhood and paved streets.

Mr. Pruitt used the basement as a workshop. It was a dark, cave-like room. Furniture in various stages of repair lay haphazardly around, and a work bench with tools organized by function that only Mr. Pruitt knew, took up the back of the room. Even though they had never said it, they always felt at ease down there. When they entered the basement, they saw Mr. Pruitt working at the bench: a handsome man with a neatly-trimmed beard and glasses. He stopped working when he noticed his children.

"Hey kids," Mr. Pruitt said. "I was wondering when you would get back." He always looked more comfortable when he wasn't dressed in the tweed suit jackets with the leather elbow patches that he wore to the office. He was a psychologist.

Sam dramatically threw himself on an ancient green couch, his favorite place to crash. It was curvy and comfortable, and he could prop his feet up at one end. A yellow tabby kitten named Queso leapt onto his chest. The kitten, happy to have a family, nuzzled against Sam's face.

Abby tossed the wet leather bag onto the sawdust littered floor and plopped into a wooden rocking chair, a wool blanket covering its bare springs.

"What do you have there, Abby?" Mr. Pruitt asked. He walked over and picked it up. He set the bag on a low table. He was a notorious packrat himself and collector of anything unusual. Philip took his backpack off, the sections of his fishing rod poked out the top, and sat on a stiff wingback chair.

"Well, we made a quick stop at the antique shop down by the highway. That's where we got the bag," Philip said. "The old lady there, Margie Jean, said it belonged to Grandpa."

Mr. Pruitt eyed the three of them sprawled lazily on the furniture.

"She said this bag belonged to Grandpa?"

"Yeah. She told us she knew Grandpa and that her husband Warren used to work together."

"Margie Jean was right. They did work together, at the old railway depot a long time ago, during the big war," Mr. Pruitt said.

"She said they worked at a zoo down off of Highway 7. Was there really a zoo there?" Abby asked. She decided not to mention the sounds they heard in the woods. For now it was their secret.

Mr. Pruitt leaned back in his chair and picked up his smoking pipe from the table next to him. He filled the bowl with rich smelling tobacco, carefully lighting it with a wooden match. A puff of smoke obscured his face for a moment before drifting out the doors.

"Sounds to me like Margie Jean's memory is a little fuzzy," Mr. Pruitt said thoughtfully as he puffed.

"Let's see if we can figure out if this old thing is indeed a long lost piece of Grandpa's past." He set his pipe on an ashtray and opened the bag. Everything inside was wet and grimy. It didn't look good.

Mr. Pruitt pulled out a crumpled shirt and spread it on the table. It was a grimy navy blue button-down shirt with the word "Caretaker" embossed on the right front pocket. He found a short brimmed cap with a tarnished brass badge on the front that read, "Forest Heights Zoological Park." It was part of a uniform and it went with the cap. Mr. Pruitt had a curious expression while examining the cap with the brass emblem. It was as if he saw something that was not real. He put it on top of the shirt.

He reached into the bag again and brought out an assortment of odds and ends.

"Monkey wrenches," he announced. Abby took them and lined them up on the table.

"I don't know what this is," he said. "It looks like a big hook with a spike, but the handle has been broken off." Abby took the unidentified tool and added it to the lineup. Mr. Pruitt collected a handful of wire, screws, nuts and bolts, and made a pile. Last, he brought out a wadded up rag. As he unwrapped the mess, he felt a solid mass hidden in the folds. It was a set of keys.

"Cool," Abby said with Philip and Sam crowding around.

"Let me see those," Sam demanded, pushing even closer.

"Hold on there, Sam, my boy," Mr. Pruitt said. He dropped the rag and studied the keys.

A brass ring the size of the palm of a hand held at least a dozen keys. They were surprisingly bright and untarnished, unlike everything else in the bag. Each key was unique. Each had different shaped notches for different locks. Some had hollow ends, a few were long and thin, and some were tiny. None of them looked like normal keys. One key was even hinged in the middle and folded in half.

"They look old," Abby said.

"You're right," Mr. Pruitt said. "Some of these look really old. Maybe a hundred years or more I would think. You might get a few bucks for them at a junk store. But I can't imagine anyone would want them for reasons other than curiosity." Mr. Pruitt liked to make a buck, if he was lucky, selling the old stuff he always managed to accumulate.

"You can't sell these!" Abby said, shocked. "Margie Jean gave us these for a reason, and they aren't leaving this house."

"Her story about where Grandpa and her husband worked doesn't make sense. As far as I know, they worked for the railroad when they were young," Mr. Pruitt said. "They were both soldiers during the big war. They both came back to work at the train depot in town. Her husband was in a car accident when the railroad stopped running the line, just before the war ended. Grandpa worked as a barber the rest of his years, even after Grandma passed. He never spoke to me about a zoo," Mr. Pruitt leaned back in his chair and sighed, lost for a moment in the past. He looked at his muddy, wet children.

"Let's head upstairs, kids. You should clean up before dinner. We'll figure this out later." They got up and walked single file up the rickety wooden stairs that led to the kitchen. Abby glanced back down at the keys lying on the table.

"I wonder what they open?" she thought.

They piled upstairs into the kitchen where music blared from a radio.

"Mom!" Sam yelled. Mrs. Pruitt stood at the sink washing dishes oblivious to the arrival of her family. She stopped for a moment as if she heard them but instead she sang, "Sha la la la la la la la la!" as best she could. She wasn't half bad.

The kitchen smelled of pizza baking in the oven. All the cares in the world slipped away. Comfort food. They needed it after today. Mr. Pruitt turned the radio off, startling Mrs. Pruitt.

"What have you three been doing to get so dirty?" Mrs. Pruitt grabbed Abby by the shoulders and looked down at her pretty, smudged face. She brushed Abby's damp hair behind her ear, which fell right back in her eyes, and said, "I thought you were going to keep an eye on these two boys." Abby smiled. They looked alike. Mrs. Pruitt's hair was longer and darker than Abby's and her eyes were blue instead of hazel, but their pretty faces complemented each other.

"So much happened today, I don't know where to start," Abby said. She looked like she was on the verge of a marathon gab session, but Mrs. Pruitt stopped her. "You can tell me all about it after you kids get cleaned up and into some dry clothes. Dinner should be ready in about half an hour." They left the kitchen through the living room doorway with Sam leading the way.

As Philip entered the living room he turned and saw Mr. Pruitt opening the oven door, and Mrs. Pruitt quickly shutting it, giving him a scolding look. They went through the living room to the hallway leading to their rooms. Sam went to his room and closed the door behind him without a word. As Abby came to her room, she turned to Philip.

"We can't tell them what happened today," she said. "If we tell them, they will never let us go out there. And I think we have to find out what is going on out in those woods. No matter what."

"I agree," Philip said in all seriousness. They did a pinky swear. Their secret was safe. They just had to confirm it with Sam. Abby went to her room and closed the door, and Philip went to his. He had the biggest room at the end of the hall since he was the oldest. Several aquariums filled with tropical fish lit the room.

The aquariums bustled with movement. The fish swam excitedly back and forth at the glass, watching him. He thought of the fish as pets, and although they only recognized him because they wanted to be fed, he still found them reassuring. He liked them.

Philip went over to his dresser and pulled out a clean pair of jeans, socks and a T-shirt. After changing he settled into a bean bag on the floor in front of the largest aquarium. The tank was a giant with many fish and green with plants. It was like a window into another world. A rectangle of liquid life. The fish watched him hoping for some food. He closed his eyes.

Somebody kicked the bean bag, startling him awake. He had slept only a minute or two, long enough to dream he held on for dear life to a half submerged log in a flooded creek. Strange animal calls echoed in the fog. He sat up grabbing at nothing. Sam and Abby stood over him.

"Wake up, sleepy," Abby said.

"You must have been having a wicked dream to get so twitchy," Sam said, reenacting Philips spastic flailing. Philip rolled sideways and gave him a swift kick on the backside.

"Hey! Come on. It's time for dinner," Sam said, pulling Philip's sock off and throwing it across the room.

"Quit playing," Abby said. "I told Sam to keep quiet about the animals." Sam gave two big thumbs up.

"You know how I don't like keeping anything from Mom and Dad," she said. "I can't help but tell them everything. I feel guilty if I don't. But I think this is something we have to find out for ourselves. And soon because there may be lost animals out there, and I don't think anyone remembers them." They made a decision to mislead and even lie to their parents if they had to.

"Dinner is ready! Come and get it while it's still hot and before your father eats it all!" Mrs. Pruitt yelled to them from the kitchen. With this, they bolted through the house.

On top of the stove was what they looked forward to whenever they could get it. Mrs. Pruitt was a genius. She figured out an easy way to please them. On pizza night, she made a personal pie for each of them. They piled their plates high, filled their glasses with iced tea, and convened in the living room with their cheesy bounty.

The room was large enough for a couch, two overstuffed chairs, and a low round coffee table in front of the fireplace. In the corner there was a television set and a VCR the size of a small suitcase. Plants of all sorts lined the windowsills where at least one pet lizard had escaped seeking freedom in the leafy jungle.

They sat on the floor around the coffee table, except Mr. Pruitt who stood at the kitchen counter and ate.

"Whose turn is it to turn on the TV?" Sam asked in all seriousness, knowing it was his turn. The remote control stopped working months ago and every night one of them controlled the television for the family. Manually.

"Everyone who wants to watch the regular channel, raise their hands," Mr. Pruitt said. Everyone raised their hand except Sam. Putting on a show, he crawled over and pressed the "on" button and put on channel three.

They only picked up three local channels because Mr. Pruitt refused to pay for cable or a larger antenna. They usually watched the main station KY3, followed by the public television channel. They never watched the third one with the non-stop religious chatter.

The local evening news came on. "This is a breaking development," the pretty reporter lady announced. "I'm here with a revered town business entrepreneur and spiritual leader, Revered Jasper Newton. As you can see behind us the holy cross which graced this hillside has fallen and burned. Pastor Newton claims some local children brought the Wrath of God upon this hallowed soil. We are here to get to the bottom of the story."

Pastor Newton stood next to the reporter in the church parking lot. There was an ambulance, a fire truck, and three police cruisers at the scene.

"I truly appreciate how the community has rallied, giving of themselves to console in this time of tragedy. We have been cursed, true, but we have found a blessing this day in the outpouring of faith and monetary donations. And I have a simple message. I am a victim, we are victims. This injustice will not go unpunished," Pastor Newton looked as serene as a sunset, just as sweet as a strawberry sundae, but his eyes seemed to be looking right through the television, into their living room at Philip, Sam, and Abby.

"It does appear that your cross has met an untimely fate, but it is not clear how a few children could have made God so angry." With this, the reporter gave the camera a cheesy smile, pointed skyward, and she said, "Only He knows. Tune back in at ten o'clock for more on this developing story. Now back to our regularly scheduled program."

Philip and Abby turned to each other in surprise. Pastor Newton thought *they* destroyed the cross. It made no sense to them. Sam went on eating.

The funny home video show came on abruptly and they forgot all about the news as they laughed at the silly things other families got themselves into. This seemed more realistic than the news anyway. The rest of the evening was uneventful.

Philip, Sam, and Abby went to bed early, exhaustion overtook them, and the day faded into oblivion. The first weekend of summer vacation was over. Mr. Pruitt and Mrs. Pruitt lay in bed for awhile reading until they fell asleep. By ten o'clock that night the house was quite.

❊❊❊

5

They plotted for the first week of summer vacation, but as the days passed the need to find the zoo began to fade. Summer took hold of Philip and Sam. Abby was still obsessed and could not let it go.

Philip and Sam spent their days riding their bikes and hanging out with their friend TC at his house playing video games and watching television. TC got every thing he wanted for some reason, but he didn't have many friends. Abby tagged along sometimes when she wasn't busy at the library down at the town square. She was on a mission to find out about the Forest Heights Zoological Park. In the beginning, she didn't find much useful information during her library visits. Then one day Mrs. Wilson the librarian led her upstairs to a room she had never been to before.

Mrs. Wilson led her upstairs, across a balcony with a good view of the main floor. Abby stopped and peered over the edge of the railing into the library lobby. She looked down at the glass entrance doors, at the checkout counter, and the tops of shelves. No one noticed her up there.

"Now Abby, you asked me about the history of Forest Heights," Mrs. Wilson said. "People generally don't care about such things. Usually, they want to know about the latest romance novel or even worse, fantasy and science fiction. Truly tasteless." Her expression turned sour as if she just bit into a lemon. "That is why I am letting you use this room. You seem to have good judgment. You can use it for the day."

"Thank you, Mrs. Wilson," Abby said.

Mrs. Wilson opened the door and stepped into the darkness. A light flickered on illuminating a room filled with books. A study table sat in the middle.

"You can stay in here as long as you want." She gave Abby a motherly librarian smile and left the room closing the door behind her. Alone at last, she took her book bag off her shoulder and put it on the table. She pulled a chair from under the table. When she sat down it squeaked loudly and lurched backward, threatening to topple her out, but she quickly grabbed the edge of the table and steadied herself. Now it was down to business.

Abby thought about what she knew. *Margie Jean insisted there was a zoo at Forest Heights a long time ago. Something bad happened at the zoo and her husband Warren died in a car crash. Grandpa worked with him at the zoo and almost died in the crash too. Dad said Grandpa and Warren worked at the train depot downtown until the end of the second world war. But he also said they fought in the war.* She wondered who was right and who was wrong. *Did a zoo really exist, or was something going on at the train depot?*

She stared at the shelves filled with books not knowing where to begin. She lay her head down on the cool table. The air conditioning whirred gently above circulating cool air through the vents in the ceiling. She felt like taking a nap.

She let out a loud sigh and leaned back in her chair. Immediately, the chair gave way and she fell backward with her arms and legs flailing out. She landed on the floor, her heart beating fast with the breath knocked out of her. She laughed out loud at herself.

"What am I doing here?" she said to herself. Then she saw a book stowed away at the back of a shelf. Sometimes a different perspective of your surroundings gives you a different perspective.

She rolled off the chair and went to the shelf with the hidden book. She pulled books from the shelf and stacked them on the floor. The mysterious book fell out onto its side with a thud and a wisp of dust. She sneezed, grabbed the book, and placed it in her lap.

It was a heavy leather-bound book with worn edges. On the cover, in large formal print it read, *Forest Heights Zoological Park, A History: 1870-1936*. She moved her hand over the cover feeling the letters pressed into the leather. This was what she hoped for. She opened the ancient volume. A stiff leathery creak greeted her. A circular emblem was stamped into the first page. It read, "This Tome Belongs to The Extraordinary Library of Thomas Meanwell".

She flipped through the book and saw black and white pictures of zoo animals of all kinds. There were pictures of buildings and animals in cages and people in funny old clothes walking through the zoo on every page. Her heart leapt. She stopped on a page of a black and white photo of the entrance to a place that she now knew existed. The stark image of a metal sign arching over a massive wrought iron gate read, "Forest Heights Zoological Park."

She could not believe it. The right side of the gate stood open, the left closed. A small baby black bear sat behind the iron bars of the left gate with his head and front paws sticking out.

"He looks sad. This wasn't his home, not his real home, anyway. He wants to escape. To go home," she thought. Even with these thoughts, Abby felt vindicated. She now had proof!

The caption under the photo read, "Bub the Cub Guards the Gate. 1917." It had been close to seventy years since this picture was taken. She noticed a man dressed in a uniform standing on the far right edge of the photo. Expressionless, the man looked across the entrance at the baby bear. Bub the Cub looked more like a prisoner than a guard. Abby felt sad again.

Seeing the guard in the photo reminded her that her grandpa may have been in that same spot looking equally expressionless at some other animal.

"He could be in a photo somewhere," Abby thought. "Maybe not in this book, he worked there in the 1940's, not the 1930's."

She opened the book to the front page with the stamp of the previous owner, Thomas Meanwell. On the wall she noticed a picture in an elaborate frame. It held the painting of a clean cut, distinguished man in a suit, with his chin up, handsome and arrogant. A small brass plaque on the frame read "Thomas Meanwell Born 1880 Died 1939." Now Abby had a face to the name that belonged to the book. She thought he must have been an important person for him to have his books and his portrait in the library.

She sat back down at the table, making sure not to tip over again. Then she did something she never did before. She shoved the book into her bag and zipped it up. She told herself that it wasn't stealing, convinced she would return it. She still felt a twinge of guilt. She couldn't say why she didn't just go downstairs and check the book out. Too many questions.

She slung the book bag over her shoulder, turned off the lights, and shut the door behind her. Walking along the balcony, she glanced down at the lobby again. There were more people now. The sound of pages turning and considerate whispering drifted up. With her new found treasure, she went down the staircase to the first floor and left the building by the side entrance closest to the stairs, like a fox leaving the hen house.

6

Philip lay on a blanket with his arms behind him, propping himself up to watch the crowd. People milled about on the fresh mowed lawn overlooking the central park of Forest Heights. The sky took on a golden glow as the sun began its evening descent. It was the Fourth of July and only an hour or so until the fireworks. The whole family drove down here in Dad's two tone blue and white FJ55 Land Cruiser wagon to gather with the rest of the town folk and see the show.

Philip had a good view of the crowd from his spot on the high terrace overlooking Crooked Creek as it meandered through the park. A bridge to his right spanned the creek. People stopped to look at the ducks and geese swimming in the water below as they strolled along the bridge. On the far side of the creek, the park spread out. Families staked out claims on the lawn, laying blankets on the grass. The swings and teeter totter and jungle gym were crawling with kids.

The old train depot, a sturdy brick building turned into a museum of sorts, was at the end of the park. Last minute adjustments to the fireworks were made in a parking lot away from the crowd. Philip spotted Abby and Sam making their way toward the train depot weaving in and out of the crowd.

Philip cupped his hands over his eyes to block the glare of the setting sun. He looked around for his parents. They were nowhere in sight. He turned back to Abby and Sam.

At that moment, Philip felt something he had never experienced before. True fear. It washed over him. His stomach clinched, and his mind raced. He saw Pastor Newton walking quickly toward Sam and Abby. They did not see him.

Philip took off at a run toward the bridge. Quite a few people walked along the bridge, and he dodged in and out between them.

He crossed the bridge and ran down the side of the grassy hill into the greater park. In the glow of the setting sun, he caught a glimpse of Pastor Newton banging on the depot's main entrance door trying to get in. No one in the crowd appeared to notice his strange behavior.

Philip didn't know what to do, but by the time he got to the building Pastor Newton was nowhere to be seen. Philip ran around to the other side of the train depot looking for another way in. He looked around the corner and saw no one. He tried the door handle at the back entrance, but it was locked. He pressed his face against the window glass and looked in, knocking lightly on the door. He could see down a short hallway into the large main room filled with glass cases and a maze of large panels covered in black and white photos. He saw no sign of Abby or Sam.

He knocked again. His heart pounded. Sweat stung his eyes. Then he saw Sam, close to the floor behind one of the large panels. He looked worried but he smiled at Philip. Sam half-crawled, half-ran to the door and pushed the release bar. Philip slipped in, and he closed the door tightly making sure it locked.

"Where did you come from?" Sam whispered.

"I saw that wacko following you. I thought I would save you guys," Philip said. It sounded funny when he said it, and they both laughed.

"You should've seen it. That crazy old guy grabbed my arm. I didn't even know he was there. Abby kicked him in the shin and luckily we got inside," Sam said. "Lucky for us the maintenance door was propped open. He banged on the door then gave up. I think he ran out of steam."

"Where's Abby?" Philip asked.

"Oh, she thinks she found something for her big zoo mystery. She's downright obsessed with that zoo," Sam said.

"Hey wingus, dingus, get over here," Abby said, poking her head out from behind a panel. "Follow me." She disappeared when she got their attention.

They followed her around a few panels with photos of old houses and expressionless pioneer families. No one seemed to smile back in the old days. She led them into an annex of the museum.

Abby showed them a large photo hanging on the wall. A caption on the frame read, "All Aboard, Last Day of Operation, August 9, 1945." The photo was of this building and a train with steam billowing from its smoke stack. The people in the photograph, dressed in their uniforms, seemed to look out of the picture at them. There were conductors, ticket sellers, workmen, waiters, and for some reason military personnel.

"Cool picture, Abby, but don't you think we should get out of here?" Philip said.

She was flabbergasted. "You don't see, do you? Look at the train cars and look closer at the people."

Philip looked again at the line of train cars. Some of the flat ones carried army jeeps, trucks, and a tank. That was strange. His jaw dropped when he scanned the last few cars. Abby laughed at this. She understood his reaction.

"I don't believe it," he said.

"What?" Sam was a little confused, and then he saw it, too. The photograph in front of them proved once and for all that Abby knew what she was doing. They never doubted her again. They became true believers.

In the photo, they saw their grandpa in a uniform just like the one they found in the leather bag. Next to him was another man who was most likely Margie Jean's husband, Warren. The children smiled. Seeing their grandpa in this photograph amazed them.

What really astonished them was that they stood in front of the first of six open-sided train cars crammed full of exotic animals. An elephant nosed their grandpa with its trunk and a giraffe, with its head bent down over the car railing, stuck its tongue out at Warren.

The animals were obviously very fond of the two men. What a sad farewell. The animals were being shipped away.

"What's going on here?" Sam said.

"I'm speechless. You were right all along, Abby," Philip said. "You're awesome!"

"I know," she said knowing that her weeks of research and determination had paid off. "Isn't this fantastic!"

Philip saw him first. Pastor Newton stared at them through the window.

"He's seen us!" Philip yelled.

"Boy, he looks mad," Sam said.

"What do we do now?" Abby asked.

"He still can't get in, or he would be in here already," Philip said, trying to remain calm.

Pastor Newton's cracked voice filled the room, raising the hair on their necks. The air seemed to leave the room like a vacuum.

"I know your kind," he said. "Always causing trouble, lying, I know because I was like you." He peered through the window. "If I had my bulhook I would teach you a lesson. And I'm not afraid to use it on some no good kids that won't do what they are told!" His eyes rolled back in his head for a second and his face contorted. "It's so dark in there. I see you though, all those beady eyes staring. I won't go back. Not ever. I taught him a lesson! It was his fault for not listening! I let the bulhook speak for me!"

Pastor Newton ended his bizarre speech and stared blankly through the window just a little longer. Then without saying anything, he turned and wandered off into the park.

"Did you see that?" Sam blurted. "I better check my underwear 'cause I think I just dropped a duce."

"Well, we can probably leave now," Philip said. "Maybe his brain short-circuited. He probably doesn't even remember why he was after us in the first place. I guess that's why he acts so weird. He's completely mad."

"Anyone want to leave?" Sam asked.

Sam walked over to the main door, opened it, and went on out. Philip followed. Abby lingered in the room for a moment longer, studying the photograph of her grandpa frozen in time standing next to, of all things, an elephant and a giraffe. An idea began to take shape in the back of her mind. She knew where to go. Now, she had to figure out when.

"Come on, Abby." Philip reappeared in the doorway. "Let's get a move on. It's about to get dark."

They walked out into the park and blended into the crowd. They did not see Pastor Newton again. They made it to the bridge spanning Crooked Creek. Half way across a loud "Boom!" startled them. The fireworks had begun so they stopped to watch. Giant bursts of color exploded over the crowd. The yearly display of patriotism had begun.

They were as awestruck as everyone else in the park. The bright colors, the loud booms and crackling blooms of fire gave them a sense of community. Everything felt perfectly fine for a moment.

Unknown to them, below the bridge they stood upon, three pairs of eyes watched them. Those eyes belonged to three shadowy figures hidden in the dark at the water's edge. The eyes reflected the light from the fireworks above, never blinking, just watching.

They found their way back to their place on the lawn. Abby sat on the blanket while Philip and Sam rested on the grass.

"Where have you kids been?" Mrs. Pruitt asked.

"We were down at the park," Philip said.

"Yeah, we weren't doing anything wrong," Sam chimed in.

"Well, that's good. Ya'll ready to pack it up and head home?" Mom asked.

"Yes!"

* * *

7

A few weeks later, Abby lay on her bed staring at the ceiling. The open windows let air into the room on this hot night. The fan, sitting at the foot of her bed, helped a little. Heat lightning flashed in the moonless sky. Listening to the cicadas chirping in the trees while trying to fall asleep, she heard a strange "click clack, click clack" on the street outside her window. She lay there as still as possible, not breathing. The noise grew louder. Something walked up the street, and she knew it was headed to the house.

She rolled off the bed and crept to the window facing the street below. A street lamp at the corner glowed, illuminating the edge of the yard. The sound of leaves crunching made her tense. Something crept around in the yard. She peered intently at the bushes next to the house. She gasped when she saw the small zebra step from the shadows. She recognized it instantly.

She opened her bedroom door carefully. It squeaked a little and echoed down the hallway.

She crept through the house, barefoot and dressed in a tee shirt that said "Snug as a Bug" and her favorite bedtime pajama pants, trying to stay on the rugs that covered the wooden floors and avoiding the areas she knew that creaked. She paused at the kitchen door that led out into the backyard. Carefully, she unlocked it, turned the knob, and opened the door just enough to squeeze out into the night air without making too much noise.

With her arms held out in front of her, she pushed aside the overgrown pampas grass lining the walkway leading to the street. It was more overgrown than she remembered so she decided to crawl. Her clothes got dirty and her skin itched from the long blades of grass that brushed against her. Sweat ran down her face.

She broke through tall grass into the yard and crouched motionless. The cicadas chirped in the trees, growing louder and louder by the minute. The heat lightening flashed in the sky; she found it difficult to breathe with the heavy humidity. She felt like she was being cooked in a pot of beef stew, which irritated her since she did not ever, never ever, eat beef. To her, cows were for petting not eating.

The baby zebra that she thought washed away in the flood appeared before her. She rushed up to it and immediately wrapped her arms around its neck. The zebra did not move a muscle. She buried her face into its mane and smoothed its back with her hand. She was in baby animal heaven. This was her dream come true. To hold and care for such a small lost, defenseless animal was her one true purpose in life. She knew that.

A strange feeling crept over her. The soft fuzzy hair on the zebra's cheek suddenly felt coarse and irritating. The fresh baby animal smell, like a puppy's belly, now smelled pungent. The baby zebra gave off a sickly sweet smell of decay.

As she pulled herself away from the animal, gobs of hair and skin stuck to her arms and face. The smell of putrescence overwhelmed her. Horror pierced her heart and swept aside all thought. She scrambled back collapsing on her back. She tried to get up. Not believing her eyes, she screamed. But no sound escaped her lips.

With skin and fur oozing off the poor animal, it walked up to Abby and put its face very close to hers.

"Help us," a thought pleaded in her head. A look of pain crossed over the animals face as flesh fell away fast, exposing the bone underneath. In another moment, the zebra vaporized in front of her and nothing remained. No fur. No bone. Not even the putrid smell. She felt her face for the flesh that must be there, nothing. Suddenly, only the deafening sound of cicadas chirping in the trees seemed real to her.

She jumped up to run back into the house and became tangled in the pampas grass. Thrashing to get away, she woke up with her sheets wrapped tight around her. She got out of bed and stood, confused and sweaty and tried to make sense of what she dreamt. She launched herself to the window; the yard looked the same as it always did. The warm summer night air fluttered into her room.

"It was just a dream," she said and returned to her bed, sitting and watching the shadows on the walls. Absentmindedly, she began to chew her fingernails. She thought about how real the dream felt. The way the fur and flesh had clung to her face made her shudder.

She quit biting her nails. She felt her face for stray hairs or anything gross, nothing. She pulled the bed sheets around her and laid her head on the pillow and stared at the ceiling. Ever since they had made their plan to go find the zoo, her dreams became more intense. She needed rest. Their fool-proof plan started tomorrow. Just like that. The chance had presented itself, and they were taking it.

The coolness of the pillow on her cheek calmed her racing mind. She imagined how great it will be when she gets to the zoo. All the animals will welcome her, and they will be so happy that she is saving them. These thoughts took on a life of their own. Abby returned to dreamland. Her grand plan would have to wait till morning.

8

Philip crawled through a well-constructed fort draped with sheets and blankets held together by an internal structure of furniture and sofa cushions. He heard laughter ahead as he brushed aside a blanket that covered a mound of stacked chairs. He entered a cramped grotto at the center of the fort with a television at one end like a shrine. Abby and Sam sat with their friend, TC, who they easily managed to convince to help with their plan. They were busy playing Mario Brothers.

TC, short, thick glasses, with a head of cow-licked blond hair, sat unblinking in front of the television, hands tightly gripped on the controller. TC could play a perfect game. Philip turned the television off with the remote control.

"Hey!" Sam yelled. TC kept on playing. Abby turned the television back on. TC finished the level with no problem. He didn't even need to see the screen.

"The Force is strong with this One!" TC said.

"Take it easy," Philip said. "You aren't a Jedi."

"Geez chill out," TC said. He waved his arm in front of him. "These are not the nerds you are looking for." Philip ignored him. "That only works on the weak-minded."

"Did you get everything?" Abby asked Philip.

"Yeah, it was pretty easy. TC's parents must buy everything they see because I found more than enough supplies." Philip said. "We can stay out for a week if have to."

"I put our packs upstairs. I think we have everything we need: food, flashlights, camping gear, and Abby's stuff." Abby's stuff included the ring of keys and her book from the library, which had a map of the zoo grounds.

TC's parents had decided to go out of town for a three-day weekend to some kind of church seminar called Arkansas Awake/Diversify your Portfolio with Jesus—A No Risk Investment Opportunity. TC's older brothers, Pat and Carl, promised to watch the house, but they took off as soon as their parents were gone.

Philip, Sam, and Abby convinced their parents to let them stay with TC until Sunday. It sounded good to Mr. and Mrs. Pruitt. They liked the idea of spending a few days together not worrying about the kids. Unaware that there wouldn't be any adults around, Mr. and Mrs. Pruitt gave them the go ahead.

"We can leave first thing in the morning," Philip said.

"I don't think I'll be able to sleep at all tonight. I think we should go right now. Get a head start. It would be fun," Abby said. She was anxious to leave. The time had come to abandon the video games and the comfortable fort.

"I'm all for leaving now," Philip said. "I think we're ready and frankly I don't want to spend all night here."

"Yeah, let's go," Sam said. "I'm wide awake. And I'm tired of TC beating me at these games."

"TC, what do you think?" Philip asked.

"I feel a disturbance in the Force," TC grinned at Sam and Abby. He grabbed the remote and turned the television off.

Philip led the way, crawling back through the furniture fort maze. They went upstairs into the real world.

They entered the foyer upstairs. TC's family was well off so they could afford a foyer. It was dimly lit. The black and white checkered tile floor made Philip think of a giant chessboard. The kitchen light was on.

Half way across the room, several dark shadows blocked the kitchen entrance. Someone yelled, "Nerds!" Abby let out a squeal.

"Scared ya, losers!" Carl yelled. Carl was tall, skinny, and his curly hair grew out into a goofy poof that almost distracted from his wispy moustache. He looked like a q-tip wearing a clown wig. Pat looked just as silly. He had black hair, perfectly combed down around his ears and forehead like a bowl. He was as thin as his brother.

They must seem cool in some world because they managed to get girlfriends. The girls were occupying the kitchen. Anne and Dee both had frizzy bleached hair with giant bangs. They were cute, girly, and wearing short skirts and colorful blouses and trying to look older than they were.

"Leave them alone, Carl!" Anne said.

"Yeah! You two are such jerks," Dee said. She pulled Pat to her.

"Man, maybe if I got me a three stooge's haircut, I could get a girl," Sam said.

"Shave your head bald and see," TC said.

"And what are you losers doing tonight?" Carl asked, jumping up to sit on the kitchen counter.

"We're going on a bike ride," TC said.

"Is that all? I saw your backpacks in the garage stuffed full of junk. What are you really up to?" Pat asked.

"If you really want to know, we're going camping," Abby said.

TC's goofy brothers burst out laughing.

"Oh yeah! Like where?" Pat asked.

"None of your business," Sam said. "We're just on our way out. Please excuse us ladies." He winked at the girls. The four of them walked out of the kitchen through a door leading to the garage. Pat and Carl glared at them while their girlfriends giggled.

"That was smooth, Sam," Abby said.

"Yeah, the ladies like it when you're confident and assertive," Sam said without a hint of sarcasm.

TC pressed the button that opened the garage door. The sound of cicadas in the dark tree tops filled the air. They put their back-packs on and rolled their bikes out into the summer night.

Fwoosh! Bang! Bright lights exploded all around them. Howls of laughter erupted from the garage. Pat and Carl aimed roman can-dles at them, shooting fireballs in all directions. Carl launched a pack of jumping jacks at them, which buzzed in the air and exploded. The sulpher smoke was gagging.

"Retreat!" TC yelled. Too many war video games had filtered into his

subconscious. "Enemy fire in sector seven! We need backup now! Copy! Over!"

They scrambled onto the street. Carl and Pat laughed hysterically sending bottle rockets flying after the disappearing bike riders.

As soon as it started, it was over. They flew down the hill. Panic changed to calm as the wind rushed at their faces. They were free. Philip led the way. He glanced back to make sure everyone followed. He pointed down the street and made a sideways motion with his hand.

They turned in unison at the bottom of the street. They glided like a flock of birds. A few street lamps and porch lights lit the street. They didn't need the lights. They knew these streets like they were in their own backyards.

They raced on and arrived at their destination. Philip, Sam, and Abby glided to a stop. But TC hit the brakes hard and swerved off into the bushes to avoid hitting his friends. He disappeared into the darkness with a loud crash.

There was a moment of silence.

"Oh, geez," TC mumbled. "I think I'm experiencing a butt malfunction. I think it's broke."

Sam burst out laughing.

"Hush," Abby warned. "His idiot brothers could be following us. We have to get out of here before they ruin our plans."

"Sorry, but that was funny," Sam said.

They got off their bikes and walked them into the dark woods looming just outside the reach of the street light. They found the trail they were looking for.

TC staggered onto the trail pulling his bike behind him. The front tire rim was a little bent, but it was still road worthy.

"Where have you been?" Sam asked.

"I was unconscious," TC said.

"We aren't far from the campsite," Philip said. He pulled a headlamp snuggly onto his head; the bright light lit the trail.

"Let's go camp!" Philip urged them on. They spurred their bikes on and they were off. The glow of Philip's head lamp cast light far down the lonely trail that traced its way through the dark wood.

They followed Philip and the fuzz of light ahead of him, their bikes clanked and bounced along, brakes squeaked when they had to slow down quick. They veered off the trail and blazed up to a giant cedar tree. Philip held aside a low limb allowing enough room to pull their bikes under. Once they were in, he let the limb fall back into place, shutting the night out.

One by one they lay their bikes down under the tree. It was a good spot. No one would notice their hiding place.

"We can leave the bikes here. I don't think anyone will find them. I think we're the only people in town who have been here in years," Philip said. "Our camp is just down the hill on the other side of the trail."

Philip led the way. They emerged from the tree, leaving the bikes and they crossed into the woods to where the hill dropped down into a steep valley. They scrambled down the slope, loose rock tumbled at each step, tough little trees helped steady them on the way down.

The sound of rocks scattering and leaves crunching echoed in the still night. At the bottom of the hill, a rocky stream gurgled. When they last passed by this little valley, the stream had roared from the torrential rains. Now the stream flowed gently and they crossed easily.

Sam broke away and took off toward the campsite. TC followed even though he didn't know where Sam headed. Philip and Abby watched them merge into the ghostly landscape.

Tall trees with large vines draping from them loomed overhead. The canopies formed a wilderness cathedral. Sam and TC reached the campsite, and Philip and Abby saw their figures dimly lit by the moon among the ruins of long abandoned buildings. A few walls still stood, with profiles that stretched upward into the night.

Abby turned to Philip. "This place is great, even though it's a little creepy." They raced each other up to the ruins.

Sam and TC stood in the middle of a concrete foundation, no roof overhead, and sections of brick walls that looked ready to fall at any moment.

"Good spot to camp, huh," Philip said. "The gear is stashed nearby. Sam, you and TC get some wood so we can start a campfire. We'll go get the gear."

Sam and TC jumped off the edge of the crumbling foundation in search of firewood.

"If they bring any wood back, I'll be completely surprised," Abby said.

"Hey, we heard that!" Sam yelled from the darkness. A loud "crack" echoed through the woods. "Found some wood!" Sam yelled.

Ignoring them, Abby followed Philip past a doorway leading out beyond their camping spot.

Weaving through a maze of crumbling brick and concrete walls, they found a small building. Philip went in and Abby peeked after him. She saw him move a large sheet of rusty metal away from the wall. Behind it were two green canvas duffle bags. He slung one over his shoulder and handed the other to Abby.

"Why are these so heavy?" Abby asked.

"Do you want to sleep in the leaves, under a log, or do you want to sleep comfortably like a normal person?" Philip asked. "These are our sleeping bags and a few extra things."

Back at the campsite, a mass of branches lay on the concrete pad. Sam and TC sat on either side of a pile of sticks pretending to warm themselves next to a nonexistent fire.

"Light this puppy up," Sam said when he saw Philip.

Philip and Abby lay the gear down, and Philip brought out a small pack of wooden matches from his backpack. He struck one and lit the pile of tinder in the middle of the sticks. It lit quickly and soon they enjoyed the glow of the campfire.

They unrolled the sleeping bags stored in the duffle bags laying them close around the fire and settled in for the evening. It didn't take long for Sam and TC to start arguing.

"No, that's not true. You don't know what you're talking about," TC said.

"There's no such thing as the Force," Sam shot back.

"But Yoda said...," TC started but was interrupted.

"I know. The Force surrounds us. You keep saying it, but it still doesn't mean it's true!" Sam said.

"I use the Force all the time!" TC said.

"You mean you can move stuff around just by thinking about it?" Sam said.

"Look here," Sam held up a corn nut snack. "If you can take this delicious nacho cheese corn nut from my hand, you can have the rest of them." Sam taunted him.

TC looked intently at Sam's hand. He held up his right hand and focused his will upon the unnaturally orange fried kernel. Sam started to look a little concerned. Even Abby and Philip began to pay close attention.

Out in the woods, a twig snapped. The noise stopped the cicadas chirping in the trees. TC saw this as an opportunity and with his left hand he flicked an ember from the fire at Sam. Sam dropped the corn nut, and TC quickly snatched it up.

"That's right!" TC said enthusiastically. "The Force works in mysterious ways! Now give me those corn nuts."

"Not fair! I was distracted! Plus all you did was to try to burn me!" Sam yelled. "I won. So give them to me." TC demanded, getting a little frustrated. "Here!" Sam tossed the bag over to TC harder than he meant, hitting him on the forehead. Sam laughed.

"Quit playing with your corn nuts," Sam said.

"You're a nerd," TC said.

"I know you are, but what am I." Sam replied.

"Shut up you two." Philip said. He stood up and looked out into the woods. He walked over to one of the collapsed walls that surrounded their camp and peered into the dark.

"Everyone heard that noise, right?" he asked looking back at them. They sat silently by the fire.

"Yes," Abby said. "What do you think it was?"

"The wind," Philip said. "Or TC's brothers followed us."

"There's no wind." Abby said. The fire crackled.

"Ow!" Philip yelled, rubbing the top of his head. A big fat cicada the size of a mouse landed on the ground next to him. He bent down and picked it up by the wings. It made an awful screeching noise as it tried to fly away.

"Nobody panic," Philip said in a fake authoritative voice. "Nothing to see here. Just a rogue bug." He held it up for them to see. Philip tossed it into the air and it flew away making that loud chirping noise.

"I'm going to bed," he said. "It's late, and we have to get up as early as possible tomorrow."

Abby pulled her sleeping bag open and got inside. Sam and TC did the same. Philip stretched out on his sleeping bag, laying his head on his backpack. It was lumpy but comfortable. He felt sleepy. It had been a long day.

He watched as Sam closed his eyes. TC emptied the bag of corn nuts into his mouth, crunching away. He fell asleep with the empty bag in his hand. "We could ditch TC in the morning," Abby whispered to Philip. He didn't realize she was still awake. He rolled onto his side to face her.

"He's loud, and he smells like corn nuts.' she said.

"I think he might ditch himself. He's pretty clumsy," Philip said.

She leaned closer to Philip. "No really. I think he may get in the way."

"What do you mean?" Philip asked.

"TC is always messing around, and he doesn't pay attention. He could get us in trouble," she said.

"Maybe, but we need all the help we can get," he said. "We don't even know where we're going, really."

"I showed you the map. The pictures," Abby said.

"Calm down," Philip said. Abby looked tired. "Go to sleep."

"But," she started to say something.

"No buts. I promise we'll figure it out," Philip said trying to be reassuring. Abby lay back on her sleeping bag.

"'Night," she said.

The bright moon cast a glow upon the woods. The stars were unimaginably far away. The embers of the fire, glowing orange and ashy, slowly died away. Out in the woods, just beyond the camp, three pair of eyes glinted in the light of the moon. The eyes watched the children sleep for awhile. Then the short, yet svelte, figures turned and shuffled off, leaves crunching under their stiff, stubby legs and black claws. Abby's eyes fluttered at the noise, but she did not wake up. They slept while the moon passed over the hills, and the sun rose over the valley.

9

They woke up early with the sun, grumpy, and noses full of campfire smoke. After a quick breakfast, they stowed their camping gear back where it belonged. They scrambled out of the valley and retrieved their bikes hidden under the cedar and continued the journey.

Sam led the way followed close by Philip and TC. Abby kept up. Her bike was made for girls with swooping handle bars and a banana seat. She liked it. It did two things, stop and go. The boys had tough bikes that went fast.

She decided to sit back and coast. She watched the boys weave back and forth down the trail stretching off through the woods. She recognized the trail from that day when they walked home. As quick as she remembered that day it was gone and so was her familiarity of her surroundings.

Her shoelace wrapped itself tightly around the bike peddle. It felt like her foot was going to pop off. She dodged a tree and crashed to the ground.

"Hey! Wait for me!" She yelled watching them disappear down the trail. "Perfect. If it's not one thing it's another." She focused on her tangled shoelace.

After an eternity she freed herself. She jumped back on her bike and took off after the inconsiderate boys. Then she came to a fork in the trail.

"Great! What now?" She made a decision and took the left path, heading downhill. A smile crept across her face. She imagined catching up to them and giving them a good thrashing for leaving her behind. She had a few sharp and witty comments ready.

The trail leveled off at the bottom of the hill and she had to pedal again. There was no sign of the boys. A twinge of betrayal crept into her thoughts. The quest had just begun and it only took a morning bike ride to ruin it. Then something caught her eye.

"Oh, it's a turtle!" she said out loud, distracted. The bike bounced suddenly across a livestock guard that lay over the trail and rolled jarringly into the muddiest field she ever saw. Barbed wire fence hung from wood posts on either side of the guard. The trail ended in black wet mud, thick with animal tracks.

She knew the boys did not come this way. A sinking feeling crept over her. She ignored it. Her shoes sank into the stinky muck as she pushed her bike forward.

At the far corner of the field sat a run down ramshackle house. The front porch sagged, the front steps, thin boards only, propped up with flat stones, and weeds grew tall on the roof. A herd of pigs waited patiently in the front yard staring up toward the porch.

Abby froze. The hot morning air stuck in her throat. Gnats buzzed around her face. She didn't dare make a sound. Long seconds passed until she felt herself move again. She pushed her bike with all her might. Her shoes made loud slurping sounds as the black mud tried to hold her.

She paused to catch her breath behind a giant oak tree. She peeked out at the house. A giant of a woman in a pink moo-moo dress and barefoot squeezed out the front door onto the rickety porch slamming the screen door behind her. The porch bent and creaked under her weight as she admired the gathered swine.

Abby knew she had to get out of there quick. She rolled her bike onto a patch of grass that snaked its way through the mud. She tried to ride her bike, but the mud-caked tires made it impossible to go anywhere.

"Come on," she said under her breath as she fought with the mud. "Geez. You've got to be kidding me." Her shoelace was untied again.

"Interlopers!" the woman on the porch screeched. The biggest pig let out a loud "Groink!" The other pigs seemed to understand and a chorus of "Groink!" erupted. The woman cupped her hands to her mouth and let go with an inhuman guttural call. "Scweeegroinkgroinkgroinkscweee!" She called over and over.

"This can't be happening. This can't be happening," Abby repeated to herself as the pigs started toward her. She ran as fast as she could frantically shoving her bike along. "Faster, faster," she told herself. She jumped on her bike, pumping the pedals as she raced through the field, tires flinging mud in the air.

She heard the pigs thumping the ground behind her. She pictured sharp hooves and slobbering snouts with jagged fangs. She decided not to look back, afraid she'd fall off her bike. At the edge of the field, she saw Philip, Sam, and TC waving frantically at her. Putting the pedal to the metal, she raced toward them.

As the rumble of hooves closed in on her, Abby heard the pig lady call "Schreegroinkgroinkschree!" once again, urging her frenzied pets on.

"Come on! Get out of there Abby, hurry!" She saw the gap in the fence, another cattle guard; she knew the pigs would not cross it. The tires of her bike made a satisfying "thullthullthull" noise as she flew across the grate onto a dirt road. She hit the brakes hard, throwing gravel out from her back tire.

The pigs stopped at the fence, eyeing the bars of the cattle guard. The woman glared at them unable to leave her porch. Abby flipped her kickstand down and got off her bike, her heart thumping with excitement. She went to the fence and knelt down to eye level with the pigs.

The guttural call came again and the pigs became frantic. Some of the pigs pawed nervously at the guard wanting to cross, but their hooves slipped between the bars.

"Come on, Abby," Philip said.

"Right," She got back on her bike.

They hauled butt down Pig Lady's narrow dirt driveway. The further they got from the farm, the better they all felt. Abby felt a little sad about the pigs even if they almost ate her. Philip led them to a paved street and showed Abby the trail she was supposed to come down. They rode down the street to Highway 7, backtracked a distance along a sidewalk until they could see the roof of the Church of the Holy Harvest on the hill, and then crossed the highway to the low water bridge spanning Crooked Creek.

Later in the day, long after the kids had come and gone, Pastor Jasper Newton walked up steps of thin boards onto a warped porch and entered a house through a screen door. He saw his daughter sobbing as she sat on a recliner sofa chair.

"Sweetness, what's wrong?" he asked.

"You are a piece of work! If you'd been paying attention, you could' a stopped those interlopers from invading my property! They panicked my sweets!" The pig lady sobbed, hurt to her very core.

"Were there devils here?" the Pastor asked, wide eyed at the thought of intruders.

"Yes! Devil's in the form of children!" she cried.

He stood there stuck in thought, imagining devilish things.

"I'm starving!" she demanded, spoiled rotten.

He remembered why he was here. "Let me get your dinner ready."

"You better not overcook my bacon. You know I like it fatty," she scolded.

"Always extra fatty. Just the way you like it." Pastor Newton cooked for his daughter every day. She never married and had no family of her own. He felt unbearable guilt for the only precious thing the Lord had ever given him, so he did whatever she wanted.

"My tummy's grumbling!" she demanded. As he bent over the hot skillet frying the bacon fat, he wondered what devils had upset his precious daughter. He didn't like devils.

***

10

They glided across the low-water bridge over Crooked Creek, a lumpy slab of concrete with a couple of metal pipes sticking out of it for the creek to flow through. A deep pool of water backed far up the creek to the bluff they had been stuck under earlier in the summer. They knew this bridge. Abby and Sam had tracked Philip from this bridge on that rainy day. They were right back where they started.

The asphalt ran out just past the bridge turning to a rough dirt road. A dust cloud billowed out from beneath their tires as they rode. They rode until the bridge was far behind them. Abby hit the brakes and stopped. The dust caught up to them and settled. Neglected overgrown pasture of briars and weeds grew on either side of the road.

"This is it," Abby said.

"What's it," Sam said.

"The train used to follow the railroad tracks from the depot to the zoo. If we head off to the right it should lead us to the zoo," Abby said. "That's what the map in my book shows anyway."

"I don't see a railroad," Sam said.

"It's out there," Abby said. "I'm sure."

They got off their bikes and considered the best way to get through the dusty green tangle of thorns and scrub.

"Guys, I can't do it," TC said suddenly. "This is as far as I want to go."

"Come on," Sam said. "It's just some weeds."

"I'm going home. You guys can keep on with this crazy thing you're doing. I've had enough adventure."

"Well we can't force you to go," Philip said.

"You're leaving?" Sam said. "Don't you want to see the zoo?"

"Sure I do," TC said."

"Then what's the problem?" Sam said.

"There's no zoo out there," he said. "Snap out it. It's a fantasy. I'm going home and sit in the air conditioning and play video games. In the real world."

TC got on his bike and peddled back down the road disappearing in a haze of dust. Philip and Abby felt relieved he was gone, just a little, but Sam was genuinely irritated with their friend.

"At least we get to keep all the snacks," Sam said

Without another word about TC, they led their bikes off the road and began to fight through the overgrown mess. Immediately, a cloud of dust and pollen enveloped them. Every leaf and limb they brushed against released a cascade.

"Great," Sam said. "First pigs and now this." He sneezed mightily.

The pollen and dust made their eyes tear up and itch and they sneezed until strings of snot ran from their noses.

"I can't push my bike any more!" Sam said.

"Me neither!" Abby said.

They were surrounded by tough briars and they had only made it a few feet from the road.

"Okay," Philip said. "We have to leave the bikes. We can come back and get them later."

They abandoned the bikes and pushed on. Everything seemed to scratch or cut or get in their eyes, even nearly pulling their backpacks off. They finally emerged, crawling, sweating, covered in red itchy scratches and out of breath, onto the old abandoned railroad track. Triumphant.

"How did you get up here so quick?" Philip demanded of Sam who stood waiting on the tracks.

"I found an animal trail and followed it. I could've ridden my bike on it if I was about a foot tall."

"Get over it, Sam." Abby said crawling out of the brambles onto the track. "You'll see your precious bike later."

Two narrow steel rails laid over dark wood beams stretched out in front of them, cutting through a green sea of weeds and brush. Nature, slowly and surely, did it's best to overtake the tracks. The sun glared down harshly. There was absolutely no shade.

Sam quickly outpaced Philip and Abby. He concentrated, stepping on every beam that lay in front of him. He became so focused on the seemingly infinite number of beams that he forgot about his bike and his brother and sister. He stumbled on a rotten beam. He turned around expecting a laugh from Philip or Abby at his expense, but instead he was shocked to see them so far behind.

"What the heck, pick up the pace," he said to himself. He sat down on one of the steel rails, took a bottle of water from his backpack and had a drink. It felt like he was in the jungle. The heat was close to unbearable. It was the kind of day when the heat could be dangerous. Sometimes a person could lose it when it was too hot outside. Fall prey to desperate mirages. It was time to get in the shade.

Sam stood up. He watched his brother and sister walk up the tracks in a shimmer of heat. He had to find some shade. He looked up the tracks at the forest in the distance.

"If I keep on walking, I can be in those woods and in the shade in less than half an hour," Sam thought. He began walking again. His backpack shifted uncomfortably, and he thought about tossing it into the weeds. He pulled on the shoulder straps and jumped until it settled.

Watching the beams pass beneath his feet, he ignored the heat. He glanced toward the forest ahead and saw something move, something that didn't belong.

Sam watched as three stiff, black and white birds turned and waddled along the tracks into the depths of the forest. "So this is what heat stroke feels like," he said to himself. "Chasing penguins to nowhere." He decided he had to catch one.

He looked back toward Philip and Abby. They were so far away. He jumped up and down and waved his arms.

"Hey, hurry up. You've got to see this."

He pointed as dramatically as he could toward the forest. He even tried to outline the shape of a penguin with his hands.

"Slow pokes," he thought. He pulled his machete from his backpack and charged heroically after his prey.

Philip and Abby stopped to watch Sam's antics.

"What's he doing?" Abby asked.

"I don't know, but he looks really excited," Philip said.

"Either he's dancing, or he has ants in his pants," she said.

They watched Sam hold up his machete and disappear into the dark forest that waited at the end of the track.

Abby's eyes widened. "Where's he going?"

"Maybe he has to go to the bathroom or something," Philip said. Abby looked skeptical.

"What? You've never had to go?" he asked.

"Come on. He was chasing something," she said.

"I hope he has sense to wait for us," Philip said. They picked up the pace. When they arrived at the forest edge, they sat down on the tracks and rested. The canopy of the tall trees hung still over them, all green, absorbing the sun for them, letting them cool off and catch their breath. They relaxed, taking long drinks from their water bottles.

"Man, it is hot!" Abby said. "I don't think I've ever been this sweaty before." She poured a little water in her hand and splashed it on her face.

"Yeah, it's warm all right," Philip said, wiping his sweaty face on his shirt sleeve.

"Where's Sam?" Abby asked.

"Who knows," Philip said. "He just had to charge off into the woods like Rambo."

"He can't be too far. He's probably waiting up ahead," Abby said.

"You're right," Philip said. "Let's follow the tracks. If he has any sense he didn't go very far."

"Sam!" They alternated yelling into the forest while they walked. All they heard were birds chirping, bugs buzzing, and a squirrel barking mad.

They wondered at the trees. The trees were old, some were so wide it would take an entire family to wrap their arms around the trunk, most were too tall to climb. And the trees got bigger the deeper they ventured into the forest. They walked and walked.

The berm of earth supporting the railroad tracks, always level, began to rise above the forest floor as it led through lowland. Tree limbs hung over the tracks.

"I don't think there have been any trains through here recently," Abby said.

"Not in a long, long time," Philip replied, climbing over a limb.

Soon it was difficult to walk without stooping or crawling or climbing to get past the crowding branches. They continued until they reached a dead end. The tracks simply ceased to exist. It was as if they had been ripped away without a thought. Beyond was green and space.

"Game over," Philip said. They stared out over the end of the tracks.

They sat down, not sure what to do.

"Well, no sign of Sam." Philip said.

"Do you think he got this far?" Abby asked.

Philip noticed a limb lying on the ground.

"He was here. Look at that branch," Philip went and picked up the severed limb. Sam had been busy chopping at trees with his machete. Looking around, they noticed other unlucky limbs with leaves wilting in the heat.

"Where did he go?" Abby said.

They sat and pondered this question. Suddenly, the birds and insects stopped their constant twittering and buzzing.

A noise caught their attention.

Peck. Peck. Peck.

It sounded wooden and hollow.

Peck. Peck. Peck.

"What is that?" Abby said, peering off the end of the tracks toward the noise.

"It sounds like a pecking sound," Philip said.

"No kidding," Abby replied as she stood up, listening intently. Sure enough the pecking continued.

Before Philip could think of something to say, Abby went off over the dead end. He launched after her. Clinging to branches, they scooted on their backsides in an avalanche of dust and rock, crashing to the ground.

A wide clearing spread out in front of them. On the far side was a massive gray bluff, a tunnel entrance bored into it high above the ground, an upside down horseshoe. Large chunks of concrete lay at the base of the bluff, broken free from the sealed tunnel. Sand had poured from the tunnel and covered much of the clearing. It looked like a giant sand box.

In the middle of all that sand was a dried out, ready to fall down tree, with Sam wedged high up in a fork. He looked scared. Below that skeleton of a tree stood three determined penguins. The tallest, most determined penguin, hammered at the tree with its beak. Peck, peck, peck. The other two stared hard at Sam.

"You don't see that every day," Philip said.

"It's true. I knew it!" Abby said. She broke cover and charged out across the clearing toward Sam and the penguins.

"Wait!" Philip called too late.

The penguins forgot about Sam and turned toward Abby.

"Oh my gosh! They're *so* cute," Abby said, ignoring the fact that Sam was trapped up the tree.

"Watch out Abby! Don't let them get you!" Sam yelled, sounding panicked.

Abby ignored him. She marched right up to the three penguins, each stood waist high to her. She knelt down to eye level and held out her hand to the one that had been busily pecking at the tree. It seemed like the leader.

"Hello. My name is Abby." It seemed funny to be talking to the penguins, but her kindness was well received. The penguin lifted its wing in return, and the two of them shook hands.

"What are you doing?" Philip asked when he caught up to her.

"Introduce yourself," Abby said. Philip hesitated then decided they were harmless. He gently shook the wing of each bird. "How surreal is this? To be out in the middle of the woods on a hot summer day, shaking hands with penguins. Wow!"

"I think it's a trick they know. Like how you train a dog to sit or fetch. Someone trained them," Abby said. "They're friendly enough, and scruffy looking too. It's strange, but I get the feeling that they're glad to see us. It's like they were expecting us."

Philip went over to the tree to coax Sam down.

"I don't like the way that one is looking at me," Sam said, pointing at the one that pecked at the tree. "It chased me up the tree. I thought I was done for."

"How can you be so scared?" Philip asked. "They look like stuffed animals."

Sam dropped from his perch onto the sand, picked up his machete where he had dropped it, and put it back in its sheath. Philip led him over to Abby and the penguins. Sam tightly shut his eyes as he held out his hand to the birds. He flinched when he felt the birds touch his hand. Now they were all introduced.

❊❊❊

11

They ate lunch on the jumble of concrete rubble at the base of the bluff. One section was big enough for them all to stretch out comfortably while Sam recounted the story of how he chased the birds and ended up in the tree. They teased him for being scared of such innocent little animals. But Sam swore the penguins had turned on him.

Now they were back together again and everything was fine. They snacked and talked about their morning, studying their surroundings. The train tunnel far above was impressive. It had been completely closed up with concrete at one time and years of sand and mud had filled it. The seal was cracked now and broken at one corner and sand spilled out in a fan at their feet. There was no way ever to imagine what purpose this all could serve. Whether it was to keep people out or keep something in they did not know.

"Can we get to that tunnel?" Abby asked.

"I doubt it. It's too high to climb to," Philip said.

"Do you think the penguins got out that way?" Sam asked as he tried to feed a piece of beef jerky to one of the birds. The penguins didn't seem interested in food.

"That's a pretty good drop," Philip said. "The fall would have hurt them."

"You know, these little guys don't look too healthy," Abby said as she stroked one of the birds along its back. "They're thin and boney under their feathers. And that smell?"

"I figured that was you," Sam said. Abby gave him one of her deadly looks.

"Maybe that's what penguins smell like. Have you ever smelled a penguin before?" Philip asked.

for them. The birds fidgeted, dancing about on their black clawed orange feet at the sight of them.

"Why did they bring us to a dead end?" Philip said.

"I'm too tired to go back," Sam said sitting down on a rock.

The penguins hopped in single file along a shelf of rock at the bottom of the bluff, then jumped to the next ledge, then the next, and to the next before disappearing behind a curtain of vines hanging from high off the bluff.

"They're going home," Abby said.

They followed the narrow ledges, natural stair steps, under the green waterfall of vines. They saw the penguins vanish over the top of a ledge.

Half-way up the bluff, they found themselves standing in a large tunnel carved into the rock big enough to drive a car through. The penguins waited again, ready to go on.

The cool air drifting out of the darkness was stale. Through the vines they could see a vast gulf of lush green spread out below covering the entire landscape. Skeletons of trees appeared like strange misshapen green giants remade by the vines. Crooked Creek sparkled in the distance, a barrier to the all consuming vines.

"What a sight," Sam said.

"That sure is a lot of kudzu," Philip said.

"Huh," Sam said.

"The vine, it's from the jungle, people used to grow it all over before they realized it would take over and smother everything."

"Maybe someone planted this stuff to hide something?" Sam said.

"Hold on a second," Abby said to the three penguins heading into the dark unknown of the tunnel. Surprisingly, they stopped and looked to her for command. "We need to rest."

"Stay!" Sam ordered, as if they were pets—and they did.

They shed their backpacks and plopped down on the stone floor, enjoying the cool air whispering from the tunnel darkness. The bugs still searched for their meal below. Quiet minutes passed, they cooled down, the damp sweat dried off their clothes leaving faint white lines of salt, minutes more passed, heads resting on backpacks, calm steady breathing, and then snoring.

The penguins stared for awhile, and then got closer and closer wondering what happened to their wards. Penguins preferred to be formal and industrious; these kids were making them impatient.

The large penguin kicked Sam in the head. Not a hard kick, just a web-foot kick to wake him up.

"Bugs in my ears!" Sam said sitting up. "Oh, never mind. I'm ready."

They scrambled awake and chased after the penguins in a sleepy daze.

***

12

Walking in darkness, Philip's headlamp illuminated the tunnel. Shadows advanced and retreated strangely around them in the incandescent pool of light. The penguins kept a quick pace just at the edge of the light.

"This has to be an old sewer," Philip said, his voice echoing down the tunnel. "I bet when it rains, the water rushes through here."

"What if it goes nowhere? It has to go somewhere," Abby said.

"Feels like a crypt," Sam said.

The sound of their shoes scuffing on the floor echoed down into the dark passage. Claustrophobic thoughts dogged them. Time seemed to stop in the tunnel, minutes turned like hours. They had entered another world.

"This must be what it felt like to break into the Great Pyramid in Egypt thousands of years ago," Philip said. "And then discovering an empty tomb."

"I hope we find a tomb—or at least some loot," Sam said.

"We *aren't* going to find anything like that," Abby told them. "This isn't some ancient ruin, it's a sewer."

"Well, technically these *are* ruins. They're just not that old," Sam said.

Abby glared at Sam, Philip sensed trouble.

"Hey!" he said, his voice lingering too long in the dark shadows outside their circle of light. "If the two of you don't stop, you're going to get a time out."

"You can't do that, only mom and dad can call time out," Abby said.

"Mom said when you act like a baby, I can treat you like a baby."

"Hey, wait a minute!" Sam said. "Abby started it."

The leader penguin kicked Philip's leg to get his attention while the other two birds hammered terrible flaps of their wings at Abby and Sam's legs.

"That is the funniest thing I've ever seen," Sam said, laughing. "Oh these birds crack me up. Getting slapped around by some stinky old penguins. It doesn't get much better than that."

The laughs faded into the dark beyond the light and they continued.

"How much longer do you think we're going to be down here?" Sam complained. "I'm ready for sunlight and fresh air."

Philip stopped suddenly. "Hey, did you hear that?" He said, the light of his head lamp settled on a collapsed hole in the tunnel wall.

"There's something in there," Sam said.

"Go find out," Abby said pushing Sam forward, urging him on, but he would not budge.

The lead penguin waddled up to the hole and stared into the opening.

"Okay. Now that's really weird," Sam said. Abby knelt down next to the penguin and peered into the opening. Before anyone could stop her, she crawled into the hole. Philip rushed over and grabbed her feet trying to stop her.

"Hey! Hold on," Abby snapped. "Something's in here."

Dust rolled up in a cloud and settled around her as she worked. With a struggle she dragged a dirty skittish animal out into the light of the tunnel. Philip and Sam marveled.

"Well, I don't know about you, but this is the strangest day ever," Sam said.

"It's so skinny. You can see its ribs," Philip said.

Abby hugged the tiny zebra. "It must've been stuck in there for days, it looks half starved," she said.

"Why was it in there?" Sam asked. "Do you think it was scared?"

"I bet it was looking for a way back home. Poor baby," Abby said softly.

"This is the same zebra I saw at the beginning of summer," she told them. "See, I knew I wasn't crazy."

"That was over two months ago," Philip said.

"It smells just like those penguins," Sam said giving the animal a funny look.

The strangely calm zebra looked up into Abby's eyes, and she recalled her dream. She felt like she was back in her dream, holding a dead, yet alive animal in her arms while it pleaded to her for help.

"This can't be a coincidence," Abby said. "This zebra is real. It's not wasting away and disappearing."

"What?" Philip said.

"Nothing," she said.

Abby coaxed the zebra along, easily becoming protector and friend. Philip noticed a faint light ahead so he switched his headlamp off. All was dark for a terrible moment. Then their eyes adjusted and they could see by the faint light radiating down the tunnel. Sam raced toward the light with Philip and Abby hurrying behind, each step slammed and echoed on the floor, leaving the animals behind to catch up.

They discovered the source. The light shown through a metal grate in the ceiling, wonderful sunlight, warm and real. Philip jumped up and grabbed the grate. Sam and Abby stepped up and held his feet for support as he tried to push the grate open. It did not budge. Disappointed, they let go of his feet, and he dangled for a moment.

"No use," Philip said, dropping to the floor. "I don't think we can move it."

"I have to go to the bathroom," Sam said without warning.

"Well, go on up the tunnel and take care of it," Philip said.

"I don't want to go down here, it's unnatural. I want to go in the bushes like a normal person," Sam said.

"So just go," Philip said.

Sam walked up the tunnel, alone.

"Let's try the grate again," Philip lifted Abby up to the grate so she could grip the bars. Philip jumped up and dangled beside her.

"Look at me! I'm a monkey," Abby said. She hung from one arm and scratched her side while making a monkey noise. Their animal friends gathered below and watched. Abby stopped her monkey act and became very quiet.

"Something touched my hand," she said, her eyes widened. "It's got me!"

Philip let go and dropped to the floor as Abby struggled wildly trying to free her hand.

"Please. Please don't eat me! I'm too young to die! Why me!" Abby yelled.

Before Philip could react, they heard laughter coming from outside the grate. Abby got loose and fell to the floor, landing on her rear end.

"Yum, yum. Fresh monkey meat for dinner!" a sinister-sounding, yet familiar voice boomed.

"Sam you rat!" Abby yelled. "Don't ever talk to me again!"

"You can't take a joke?" Sam said, laughing. "Geez, quit being so serious for once." Abby looked hurt, she didn't like being made fun of.

"How did you get up there?" Philip asked.

"Walk up the tunnel, and you'll see," Sam said, smiling from the other side of the grate at them with the afternoon sun at his shoulder.

* * *

13

They located a side passage in the tunnel leading to a small room. Rusty metal rungs held to a wall and led to an open grate in the ceiling.

Sam looked down into the room from above. "Come on up, you're gonna like it up here!"

Abby started up the rungs and then stopped midway, "What about the animals? We can't leave them," she said controlling her urge to bolt free of the sewer.

"Take it easy," Philip said. "I've got them."

Philip wasn't thrilled about it but he picked up each penguin and handed them to Abby, who passed them on to Sam. Then he hauled the little zebra up the ladder. The animals were all skin and bones, not a burden at all, but the smell reminded Philip of moldy sour cheese. He didn't like the smell that now clung to his hands and clothes.

Above ground again, they stood together in a sprawling brick-paved courtyard. At the center of the courtyard was a fancy pavilion with a conical peaked roof. Stout buildings of brick and stone and square lines, some with fences and others with black iron cages, surrounded the courtyard. Brick-paved walkways led off in all directions and park benches were neatly arranged under huge shade trees. Far from being ruins of a once bustling zoo, this place seemed ready to come back to life. Time had been kind to the old zoo.

The sun was low in the sky, casting long shadows across the grounds. The zoo was much more wonderful than they ever imagined or even hoped for. Exhilarated, they wanted to explore every corner.

The animals were excited too. Before they could react, they watched as the little zebra pranced away down one of the wide walkways while the penguins waddled off importantly down another. The animals were home and had plans of their own.

"This is incredible," Philip said. "Abby, this day is definitely for you. If you hadn't talked us into this, we never would have known." He gave her a rough hug.

"You don't deserve a hug for scaring me like that," Abby said to Sam, but she gave him a high five instead.

Abby sat down on one of the benches and quickly took off her backpack and dug around in it until she found the book from the library. She opened it to a bare bones map of the zoo that once guided visitors around the park long ago.

"This is the most recent map of the zoo grounds I could find. It's from 1913," she told them. Philip and Sam sat beside her as she studied the map and got her bearings.

"I think we are here," she said, pointing at a small building on the map labeled Band Stand. "It matches that pavilion. And over there, toward those trees, that's where the Great Lawn is according to the map."

All the buildings around them, and those beyond, had names: Monkey House, Lion House, Great Aviary, Terrace Walk, Wolf and Fox Dens, Elephant House, Giraffe House, Refreshment Rooms, and many more. Every kind of animal imaginable once lived here, and strangely enough some still did.

"We should find a place to camp before it gets dark," Philip said, looking toward the sun that inched past the tree tops. "We must have been in the tunnel longer than we thought."

"We could sleep out on the Great Lawn," Sam said. "That sounds like a nice place." Just as soon as the idea sprouted it was gone when a deep roar from the direction of the Great Lawn startled them. They instantly knew that hair-raising roar could only be from one animal.

"That's a lion!" Abby said.

"Keep your voice down," Philip said. "We need a more secure place to stay the night." He glanced around at the buildings surrounding them, although none looked particularly welcoming.

"Let's go here. It's not that far," Abby pointed at a square on the map labeled Zoological Society Offices and Library. The building was to the north and skirted around the Great Lawn and the prowling lion. "Maybe we can find out what happened," she said.

"Any excuse to visit a library. Really, you want to look at more books at a time like this? What about the Monkey House?" Sam wanted to explore. No lion was going to deter him.

"Abby's idea is the best one. We should go now while it's still daylight," Philip said.

Abby put her backpack on and kept the book open to the sketchy map. They headed north along the brick paved walkway that matched with the direction on the map. On the way, the strange old buildings they passed made it impossible for them not to stop and want to investigate.

Sam ran up to the Small Mammals House: a solid, brown brick structure with tall, dingy windows. He tried to open the door. "Locked," he said. "But I want to go in!"

Abby told Philip to open the small pocket in the back of her backpack. When he did, he pulled out the ring of keys that belonged to their grandpa.

"I knew these would come in handy," Abby said, taking the keys from Philip. She inspected the lock on the door and after a few attempts she found the key that fit. The lock clanked, and she swung the door open. Inside was a shadowy open room with cold tile floors. The windows let in enough light for them to marvel at the rows of individual glass compartments lining the walls. Each one held masses of dried grass, bits of wood, and leaves. They heard a muffled squeak. Then another. Activity erupted within each compartment as mice, guinea pigs, hamsters, chinchillas, rats, gerbils, rodents of all kinds looked out at them from their nests. The squeaking and chittering became very loud as the warning of the strangers spread through the cages.

"They're happy to see us," Abby said, tapping on the glass belonging to a guinea pig. The animal looked bizarrely scruffy, and more irritated than friendly.

"How are they still alive?" Philip wondered.

"They like people," Sam said, making faces at a particularly irritated looking gerbil. The gerbil sniffed the air, whiskers twitching as he tried to read Sam's expression. Sam pecked and pecked at the glass with his finger until the glass cracked from corner to corner. The gerbil gave Sam the fiercest glare a gerbil could give to another at the destruction of its home. "Sorry."

After thoroughly making themselves unwelcome, they left the building in turmoil. Abby locked the door behind her just as she found it, and they continued on toward the library.

As they passed the Insect House, Sam asked, "Anybody up for some bugs?"

"No way!" Abby said. "Just the thought of what must be in there makes my skin crawl—-spiders, centipedes, beetles, grubs, worms. Gross."

They walked on making sure to stay on the main walkway. They didn't want to get lost. At a fork in the walkway, a giant wrought iron cage loomed before them: it held a dead tree and three grisly black vultures perched on bare branches.

"Whoa!" Sam said, watching the birds watch him.

"That's the Vulture Sanctuary," Abby said. "They don't look friendly."

They skirted the cage while the birds craned their necks after them. They kept walking until they came to a wooden bridge that arched gracefully across a meandering pond stretching far out of sight on either side of the bridge. To the east, a group of otters stopped playing to watch from their small island, Otter Island. A sign at the bridge read, "Scenic Leisure Pond: Paddleboat Tours at West Dock."

They crossed the bridge over the dark water and came to a wide avenue: the Grand Way, according to the map. To the left, the Grand Way led to the western reaches of the zoo. To the right, the Grand Way led east to the Main Entrance. The building that housed the Zoological Society Offices and Library was near the Main Entrance.

They went east following the wide brick lane. Long ago horse drawn buggies and automobiles with thin spoke wheels clattered and clanked busily over these bricks to visit the zoo. Now they were just memories captured on black and white photos in a book that Abby carried under her arm.

The dark waters of the Scenic Leisure Pond paralleled the Grand Way. Every other step spooked some unknown animal that would scurry away stirring the calm water, spreading ripples toward the grassy banks. Abby stopped in front of a plain two-story building of gray stone with many windows.

"This is it," she said. "I think."

They ran up the front steps to the heavy doors. Philip tried the handle, but it was locked.

"Come on," Sam said. "Why are all the doors locked in this place? No one wants in these old buildings."

"We do," Philip said.

Abby jingled the ring of keys. "We can look for another way in," she said. "Or we can just let ourselves in."

Abby tried a few keys until one slid into the keyhole. She turned it and the lock clacked back. She turned the handle, and the door swung inward.

They entered the lobby. The light faded and pinched out as the door slowly closed behind them. In the once inviting room worn out lounge chairs and magazine tables gathered dust. Everything appeared to be made of white marble, the walls, the floors. A thread bare length of red carpet pointed to the reception desk. To the left was a staircase, and beyond a hallway.

"You know, this place isn't so bad. Just a little dusty," Sam said.

"Dusty? I beg your pardon. I just cleaned yesterday," A light flared from a lamp illuminating a figure at the reception desk. Philip and Sam froze. Abby screamed.

"No need to be frightened, you scared me, too." A woman stood at the desk with a truly welcoming smile on her thin, care-worn face. She wore a smart looking uniform and hat that was a generation or two out of style. Her hair was dark and neatly-kept under her uniform hat. She seemed young, but she somehow looked different.

"Who are you?" Philip demanded.

"That's what I was going to ask you children," the woman said. "My name is Beatrice Goody. You can call me Betty. Everyone does," Betty said. "Now it's your turn."

"I'm Philip. This is my sister, Abby, and my brother, Sam."

"We didn't think there would be anyone out here," Abby said. "We thought this place was abandoned. We weren't even sure it existed until today."

"I can't tell you how delightful it is to have living, breathing guests again. I can't even remember the last time," Betty said. "What year is it?"

Sam blurted out the year.

"Oh my, so many years, decades, gone. How time passes," Betty said surprised.

"Betty, what did you mean by living and breathing guests?" Philip asked.

"Oh, you can't tell? That is a compliment," she said, absent-mindedly touching her hair. "I'm dead. Have been for years. It's not so bad, but I do miss the food."

They wanted to run away. Run as far away as possible and never come back. But they stood their ground. "You aren't going to hurt us, are you?" Abby asked, alarmed and defensive.

"Good gracious, no! Why would I do that? I haven't talked to anyone new in years." she said reassuringly. Abby felt a flutter of a kindred spirit in Betty.

"I know you children have questions, and there are answers, but evening time is here and it is fine to take a rest," Betty said. "I know the perfect place."

They followed Betty through the lobby and up a stairway to the second floor. Every step she took on the stairs was a symphony of creaks and cracks and grinding of joints. With a settling of bones she stood at a door, a brass plaque read, "Reading Lounge".

The Reading Lounge was open and airy. One end of the room had a grand fireplace with couches and a low table in front of it. Viewing windows covered a long wall and looked out onto the zoo grounds below. Shelves packed with books and odds and ends lined another wall.

Betty lit oil lamps on the mantle over the fireplace as dusk arrived. They tossed their backpacks in a pile and made themselves at home.

"Isn't this nice, children? We should have a lovely time here. I do love entertaining," Betty said. She almost looked alive in the flicker of the lamplight.

Philip unloaded a pile of snacks from his backpack over the table by the couches and they sat down and ate. Betty stood and watched.

"Is that what people eat these days?" Betty asked.

"Sure," Sam said. "Want some?"

"No, thank you. Unfortunately, when you're dead, food is a memory of dust," Betty said.

"So, if you're dead, does that make you a zombie?" Sam asked. "Cuz all the zombies I've ever seen in movies are always chasing people and eating their brains. Then you have to chop their heads off."

"Sam, be quiet," Abby said.

Betty laughed. "I'm not sure what you're talking about, but it sounds thrilling. I've never chased or eaten anyone. I just keep this place clean and look out the windows. Occasionally, I visit with old friends while on a stroll."

"There are other people here?" Abby asked.

"Oh, yes. Thomas calls us the skeleton crew. He likes to joke. And, of course, there are the animals."

"What about the animals?" Philip asked.

Betty looked at them quizzically and asked, "Did you see any animals in the zoo?" Abby told her about the penguins and the little zebra.

"Oh my," Betty said, "Those animals have been dead longer than I, and there are some still prowling about that are much, much older."

"Zombie penguins! That's awesome!" Sam exclaimed, empting a bag of chips.

"But they look so normal," Abby said, saddened at the thought of her little companions having died long ago.

"I guess that explains the smell," Sam said. Abby popped him on the shoulder for being so insensitive.

"Are all the animals in the zoo dead?" Philip asked.

"Yes, yes. But don't worry. We all enjoy it here," Betty said. "Live and let live, so to speak."

"How did this happen? It doesn't seem possible," Philip said.

"I don't know. Thomas would be the one to talk to. He is the Superintendent of the zoo. Well, he was, and sort of still is. We can visit him tomorrow. He will decide what to do with you children," Betty said unintentionally ominous.

"Why are you here?" Abby asked.

"I haven't thought about that in a long time," Betty said. "Let's see. I started work here one summer in 1929 along with my brother. We both worked at the concession stands. We had such a fun time watching the people, such crowds then, and the sounds and smells, and good humor, sweet memories. Back then I lived in town with my family and every morning I took the train to work and every evening I rode the train back to town. My brother and I grew restless and wanted something challenging to do. I took a job as a receptionist for the zoo offices, and my brother became a caretaker of the animals. We knew there were strange things going on at the zoo. Accidents would happen, deaths, and the same animals would still be in their cages for many, many years, and people too. I never paid it any mind until the military arrived and then, well, I died."

"Someone hurt you?" Abby sounded horrified.

"No, it was an accident," Betty said. "The military people with their scientists were here only for a short time, no more than a year, when the Great War really got going, but they sure made a mess of things. First they closed the zoo and then they didn't let anyone in or out. Then the animals, the ones still alive, the poor things, they were ignored, left in their cages to die to see what would happen, an experiment, so the scientists said. I can't think of a greater punishment than to be ignored to death. The animals all died, of course, but they still reside here at the zoo."

"What happened to you," Abby prodded.

"It was a silly thing, no glamour," she said. "A limb fell from a tree and hit me on the head. It was a windy day and I wasn't careful. I died and then went back to work. You get used to it."

"Our grandpa was a caretaker too," Abby said.

"What was his name?" Betty asked.

"Archie Pruitt," Philip answered.

Betty's eyes widened. "Your grandpa was Archie Pruitt? He was a wonderful man and a good friend," She looked at them, bewildered.

"What was your brother's name, Betty?" Abby asked.

"Warren," Betty said.

"That's weird," Philip said. "Was he married to a woman named Margie?"

"Yes, Margie Jean," Betty said.

"We met Margie Jean not long ago," Abby said. "She told us about Warren and our grandpa."

Betty wanted to cry, but she could not. Just one of the things not allowed after death.

"What did she say about Warren?" Betty asked brushing away the memory of tears. "Did he make it?"

"He died," Abby said.

"When did he die? I hope he had many good years," Betty said.

"Well, it sounds like he died when the zoo closed," Philip told her. "Maybe the same day? He wrecked his car. Margie Jean found him. And our grandpa was with him but he lived.

"Well, what happened?" she asked.

"Nothing, I guess, it was an accident," Abby said. "Grandpa never told anyone and the town forgot about this place and everyone along with it."

Betty sighed. Her expression turned flat, unreadable. "They killed him," Betty said under her breath.

"Children, I have to leave you for awhile. I don't want you to see me like this. I have to be alone. Have a good night sleep," Betty trembled to her bones as she left the room, closing the door behind her.

"I hope she's alright," Abby said.

"She's dead. Nothing can hurt her," Sam said.

"You could see she was hurt," Abby countered.

"That's not what I meant, geez," Sam argued.

"She knew grandpa. Can you believe it?" Abby said, ignoring Sam.

"The town must have amnesia or something to have forgotten all of this," Philip said.

"It must be the military, or the scientists, like Betty said. In movies they do stuff like that all the time," Sam said. He joined Philip at the long stretch of windows overlooking the zoo, now long past sunset and dark. Sam opened the window by turning a handle, a panel of glass swung outward into the night. Warm air greeted them, and chirping insects and frogs, and growls and roars, and splashes in murky water, and unintelligible exciting exchanges between unseen beasts.

Abby went over to listen and look. As their eyes adjusted to the night outside, they noticed shadowy trees and fireflies blinking below them. They saw buildings and what looked to be a few lamp lights swinging to and fro along the walkways.

"Those must be other people like Betty. Checking on the animals, I guess," Philip said.

"You know how close we came to having a zombie grandpa?" Sam said. Holding his arms out stiffly, he lurched stupidly back to the couches, pretending to be a zombie.

"Uuugh." he moaned as he flopped onto a couch.

Philip and Abby chased after him jumping wildly on the furniture, bouncing off cushions, and leaping from nimble footholds.

The tumbling and jumping stopped and they collapsed on the old musty furniture. They fell asleep, dead to the world.

Betty checked on them during the night, covered each of them with a blanket, extinguished the oil lamps on the mantle, and placed a black and white photograph on a table. She gazed at the picture fondly. She was young and vibrant then, sitting between her brother, Warren, and Archie Pruitt. They were squeezed onto the seat of a carriage tethered to a disgruntled looking ostrich.

"Those were the good days," Betty said to no one. She left the room, leaving her guests to a well deserved night of rest.

❋❋❋

14

Abby woke up first, the sun peaking in through the windows, blinding her even with her eyes closed. She sat up and saw the photograph on the table that Betty set out during the night. She picked it up

"It was all true," she murmured. Grandpa looked as cheerful as ever and so young. Betty and Warren looked young and happy, too. Abby thought about the tragic ends they met.

"Why didn't he ever mention the zoo?" she wondered.

Not wanting to wake her brothers, she got up quietly to investigate the bookshelves. She scanned the titles but nothing jumped out at her. She thought about lying down on the couch again and go back to sleep when she noticed a space on one of the shelves. A book was missing. An idea struck her.

As she searched her backpack, Betty entered the room carrying a silver serving tray with glasses and a pitcher of water and set them on the table.

"Good morning, young one," she said softly to Abby. Betty in the morning light took a minute to get used to. If you passed her on the street, you would think she was sick or maybe had a bad face-lift or just needed tons of moisturizer. But you could tell something about her was downright unnatural.

Abby retrieved the book she "borrowed" from the town library.

"What have you there?" Betty asked as Abby placed the book into the empty space on the shelf. It fit perfectly although it showed more wear than the others.

Betty looked surprised. "Where did you get that? That book has been missing for as long as I can remember."

"I found it hidden at the Forest Heights library. It helped lead us here," Abby replied, pleased with her discovery.

Betty touched the book, remembering something from the past.

"A very naughty boy took this book before he disappeared. He was constantly up to no good, harassing the animals, teasing people," she said. "He worked at odd jobs around the zoo, cleaning animal cages, collecting rubbish, and sweeping sidewalks. Not the most pleasant things to do, but rewarding in their own way. One day he went into a fit of rage. A little elephant named Giblet missed its mother and would not heed the boy's command. So, to make his point the boy beat Giblet with a bulhook until it died from the wounds, but mostly from fear. Giblet came back from the dead as animals do here. The boy fled the zoo in terror and was never seen again," Betty explained.

"What was his name?" Abby asked.

"His name was Jasper," Betty told her.

Abby knew immediately who Betty described. A young Pastor Jasper Newton! She felt annoyed when she the thought about the times he had harassed them. And the terrible thing he had done!

"We've run into Pastor Newton a few times," Abby told her. "He's a preacher now and he's not very nice. People in town really like him for some reason. Lots of people go to his church."

"A wicked boy becomes a wicked man," Betty said.

"Wicked is a good way to describe him," Abby agreed. "He deserves something bad to happen to him."

"Whether he deserves it or not, I don't know, but don't judge his deeds too harshly, he no doubt judged himself," Betty said. Abby was truly starting to like Betty. She was a kind woman, even though she was no longer alive.

She took the book down from the shelf and handed it back to Abby. "The book belongs with you. Now wake your brothers. We have a lot to do and see today. I haven't had this much to do in years, and with new friends, so much the better."

Once Philip and Sam managed to get up, they ate a quick breakfast from their dwindling supply of snacks. They craved real food: granola bars and beef jerky were only fun to eat every so often. They asked Betty if there was any food around.

"Not for about half a century," she said.

Abby told them about Pastor Newton. Philip and Sam were shocked by the story. "If I had been there I would have stopped him," Sam said.

"Could we take a ride on the ostrich, too? Just like in the picture?" Abby asked.

"Maybe," Betty told him. "That old bird is a bit grouchy these days. But first I want to show you around the zoo before we meet with Thomas. He may have other plans for you, and I want to enjoy your company as much as I can."

"Isn't today Saturday? We're supposed to be home tomorrow," Philip said, remaining unflinchingly practical.

"I hadn't thought about going home," Sam said.

"We can't think of that now," Abby said. "I want to see the zoo and all the animals. We can figure how to get home later."

"Thomas will know how to help us, of course," Philip said dryly. "He has all the answers, apparently."

"Now you see," Betty said.

They left the room, marched through the hallway, down the stairs, and into the lobby. From behind the lobby desk, Betty grabbed a sun hat with a wide brim.

"I try to keep out of the sun as much as possible," she told them. "For my complexion." Philip gave Abby a look and Sam shrugged.

They left the lobby and stepped out into the breezy summer morning. A few clouds floated by high in the blue sky. Betty locked the entrance door behind them with a key similar to the one Abby had used the day before.

"Why did you lock the door?" Abby asked.

"Habit I guess," she answered. "Years ago a family of mischievous otters managed to get in. They made such a mess of things. It took me days to clean up." The look of disgust on her face told them she still held a grudge.

"That reminds me, how did you open this door?" Betty asked, putting her hands on her hips.

"We have keys," Abby said. "We found them," she showed them to Betty.

Betty took the keys and studied them. "This is quiet extraordinary! These are keys to everything in the zoo. Some of these don't have duplicates and are for places none of us have been able to get to for years."

"These are the master keys." She looked puzzled.

"They look like keys to me," Sam said. "Dad said they weren't worth but a few bucks."

Betty hesitated but reluctantly handed the keys back to Abby. "Don't lose them," she told her. "We will show them to Thomas later. He'll know more. He always knows more."

"Now, what should we do first?" Betty asked, perking up.

Before they could reply, Betty answered herself. "Who would like to see the wildlife of Africa?" Abby jumped up and clapped with excitement. Philip and Sam whooped.

"That's settled then," she said with a satisfied smile.

Betty led the way. They skipped and played along the Grand Way, passing the bridge that spanned the Scenic Loop Pond, and kept westward bound. The walkway was lined with bigger than big trees and neglected flower beds. They passed buildings one after the other, some with many windows, some with high fences, and most were built strong with brick and stone. Vines crept over it all.

As they passed the structures, Betty said things like, "That is the Reptile House. Don't go in there unless you like creepy crawlies." Or, "There is the Parrot House. Very dusty birds—and noisy. They make me sneeze."

They wanted to go into every building and explore. They could barely contain their curiosity. Betty assured them that it wasn't worth the effort, that there were better things to see where they were headed.

They took a path to the right that led through a huge iron gate. They passed by a series of ponds where ghastly flamingoes and filthy swans and dirty ducks busily preened themselves, squawking noisily. Brightly colored coy lazily floated in the water, twitching out of sight at the slightest noise. In one of the murkier ponds, a giant snapping turtle surfaced, its grisly face and bulbous eyes watched them as they passed. Unpleasant smells drifted on the wind. Every animal they came upon was long dead, but each continued to live as if nothing was out of the ordinary.

The path widened into a courtyard with a formidable brick building waiting at the far side. A loud and familiar noise called to them. It was the same trumpeting they heard months ago while waiting under a bluff in the rain.

"That startles me every time I hear it," Betty said. "I think that old elephant knows we are here."

They ran toward the building, desperate to see the elephant for themselves. "Easy children," Betty said. "Follow me." She led them down a sidewalk around the back of the building.

Below was a Greek amphitheater, a half circle of concrete benches set into the hillside overlooking an enclosed space of scattered trees and a mighty mud wallow. Two of the biggest elephants they had ever seen sat on their haunches in front of a strangely dressed man.

The man gestured grandly with his arms and both elephants sat on their rear ends and lifted their front legs up, raising their mighty heads skyward. The trainer clapped loudly, and the animals stood up. He clapped again and the largest elephant lowered its head, and the man grabbed a tusk and climbed up, hoisting himself onto its back. He stood tall atop the elephant, turned to his crowd and bowed deeply. Philip, Sam, and Abby clapped heartily in appreciation of the grand show. Betty waved at the man as they walked down to him.

Up close, he was a fierce looking man, heavy dark mustache and forked beard, dark eyes under a determined brow, an intelligent face more clever than fierce. He was one of them. Dead. He wore a uniform, of sorts, navy blue almost black. It was different all together than what Betty wore. It looked older. He wore a burgundy sash around his waist under his old frock coat and a faded red fez on his head.

"You knew we were coming," Betty said to the man.

"Of course! I listen to the animals!" he replied in a drawling, heavy accent, British maybe, with hints of far away desert lands.

He turned his attention to the silent children. "I am Haji Abdu, son of Persia, humble pilgrim of Mecca and Medina, explorer and member of the Royal Geographical Society, I have traveled to the far places of the world, I called none my home, and thought no place would hold me, until I arrived here. In life and death I am bound to this land. These are my friends, Jumbo and Penny. How did you like our show?"

Abby replied first. "It was wonderful. I didn't know elephants could do all that." Philip and Sam agreed.

"What are your names and please explain how such young children happen to find themselves where they obviously do not belong?" Haji Abdu asked with a raise of an eyebrow and a grin.

They introduced themselves and each shook his hand. His skin was like dry leather pulled tight over his bones and he was wiry strong. He was like the rest of the zoo inhabitants, long dead and seemingly content with the fact.

He remembered Archie Pruitt and had kind things to say. The discovery of their connection to the zoo and the past pleased him greatly.

"Would you like to meet my companions?" Haji Abdu asked the children. They followed him into the elephant yard, his bones creaking and cracking with each stride.

"Jumbo, up!" Haji Abdu commanded. The largest elephant wound his trunk around Abby, yanked her up from where she stood and plopped her onto his back. At first she was nervous, but as soon as she patted the animal on its enormous head, feeling the contours of his skull beneath the thick rough skin, she felt fine. Jumbo brought his trunk up and touched her face. It tickled, and she laughed.

"Jumbo likes you, Abby!" Sam yelled. Abby thought so too. She could tell he was a well meaning elephant. Then she remembered she was sitting on an animal that was no longer alive. She felt sad all of a sudden.

Haji Abdu instructed her on how to get down. Jumbo raised his front leg so she could step onto it. She balanced herself by clinging to a massive ear and then she jumped to the ground at the last minute.

"You are a natural with animals, young lady," Haji Abdu said.

She smiled and then asked. "Why are Jumbo and Penny here? I mean, I know we are in a zoo, but what happened to them?"

"I think Abby wants to know why they are zombie elephants," Sam added.

Haji Abdu thought about this for a moment and laughed. "Jumbo and Penny were the stars of the zoo, when it opened and even when it closed. They both lived for only a year. The stress of being taken from their homes and moved far away ended their lives. But a strange thing happened. I think you know what I mean."

"They didn't really die," Philip said.

"They seemed as normal as could be so the show went on. Years went by and more and more animals died and came back to life. Then one day I died and found myself as you see me now. That was in 1891." Haji Abdu told them. "The public didn't notice anything was different and the zoo stayed open. Everyone was happy."

"You have been here for over a hundred years?" Sam asked in amazement. "And you kept working the whole time? I would be so bored doing the same job day in and day out."

"You would be surprised how much work there is to do when you're dead," Haji Abdu answered. "And as they say, friendship is the spice of life. And I have many friends here." He gave Penny a friendly pat on her sweet elephant face.

"So nobody thinks it's strange that every living thing that died here came back to life?" Philip asked.

"Of course it's a strange thing. But who's to say this is right or wrong? We cannot complain about this gift. It is best sometimes to take solace in the fact that there are great mysteries and unknowable answers beyond what you or I can grasp. Perhaps it is best we do not understand." The children thought about this in silence.

"Would you like to join us on our tour of the zoo, Abdu?" Betty asked.

"An adventure to raise our spirits!" Haji Abdu declared. "We will travel in a way deserving of our young guests!"

***

15

With a little help Hadji Abdu managed to harness riding platforms to Jumbo and Penny. Each platform was really a big saddle with wide seats to sit on. They climbed ladders and took a seat while the elephants waited patiently.

Once on the move, they felt like royalty. Jumbo would throw his trunk high in the air and trumpet loudly and then Penny would answer. This let the rest of the zoo inhabitants know the procession was on its way.

"This is the way to travel!" Haji Abdu said sitting atop Jumbo leading the way with Abby and Sam on either side of him. Penny followed close behind with Betty and Philip swaying side to side in their seat.

They paraded down the Grand Way into the heart of the zoo. They crossed the bridge over the Scenic Loop Pond and the otters on Otter Island leapt into the water. Instead of heading toward the Great Lawn, Haji Abdu led them westward into unexplored areas.

They encountered many fantastic things on their tour. Polar bears lounging in the shade in their dens, a savannah with giraffes and camels, and a lion and its pride, wildebeest, gazelles, baboons, and even a cheetah.

Abby nearly lost it when she saw a little zebra flicking its tail happy to be back with its mother. "That's our friend!" she said to Haji Abdu and then quickly told him every great and small detail, more than he would ever want to know, about herself and that zebra.

"You say you found him in a tunnel under the zoo?" he asked, puzzled.

"Yesterday," Abby said. "He was trying to get home."

"I've never been down in the sewers," Haji Abdu said. "If you arrived that way, you are the first. I'm impressed."

"Well, we didn't do it on our own. Three penguins showed us the way. They knew exactly how to get here."

He studied Abby's face for a moment. "You are interesting children." He stroked his beard absent mindedly, contemplating. "Strange about those penguins, seems they've been coming and going as they please," he said. "There is an unwritten rule that we are careful not to break: Keep to the zoo."

Before Abby could launch into an unending series of questions, Sam blurted, "What is that smell!"

"Sea Lion Cove!" Haji Abdu told them.

Haji Abdu halted their march at a pool filled with dark water. He whistled loudly and a sleek face poked its whiskered snout up out into the air. Another one popped up, then another, and another, until half a dozen sea lions stared at them. He signaled with his hands and the sea lions swam about, performing silly tricks in unison and waving their paws. A grand finale of flips and twists sent the foul smelling water splashing everywhere. They all clapped after the performance, and the sea lions slipped back into the murky depths of the pool with barely a ripple. The show was over.

Haji Abdu urged Jumbo onward with Penny not far behind. Just when the thrill of the sea lions was wearing off, they found themselves in a pretty courtyard with beautiful blossom-covered bushes, intricately manicured juniper trees, and a lovely fountain of green algae. Nearby a statue of a lazy fat man sat atop a boulder. At the other side of the courtyard, there was an ornate Oriental-style building.

"So peaceful," Abby said.

"This is Temple Pagoda," Haji Abdu said. "Let's see if old Chang Tzu is still with us."

They entered the ornate building with its mountain-like roof and high peaks. Haji Abdu instructed them to take off their shoes before walking on the polished wood floor. Silent socked feet padded quietly across the room to a garden filled with bamboo in the center of the building. Sunlight filtered in through a window in the roof. A pair of pandas warmed themselves in the sun.

Like big over-stuffed toys, the pandas woke up and rolled into a sitting position and scratched. Then the cutest thing happened, a little baby panda kicked out from under a pile of leaves, shook his head and sneezed.

"Can I pick him up?" Abby begged.

"I think that would be okay," Haji Abdu said.

She took the little animal in her arms and imagined she was holding a teddy bear. The little panda played with her hair and clenched its paws when it grabbed. Abby reluctantly put it down, and the little one joined the adult pandas.

"That is Hu and Yu," Haji Abdu said pointing to the large pandas. "I can't remember which one is which. The small one is Lulu."

The bright sound of a flute floated into the building from the courtyard. They rushed outside forgetting about the pandas, to the dismay of the pandas. Once out of the Temple, they found their shoes were gone. A wrinkled, goofy man with wispy hair sat cross-legged atop Jumbo. He wore a simple robe of pieced-together cloth. It looked like he made it himself. He played a wooden flute.

"Hello Chang Tzu," Haji Abdu said.

"Chang!" Betty called to him, sounding irritated. "Those are my last pair of shoes. Where are they?"

Chang Tzu stopped playing his flute and laughed. "I will give back your shoes if you introduce your curious friends to me."

"This is Philip, Sam, and Abby," Haji Abdu said. "Betty and I are giving them a tour of the zoo before heading to Thomas's place so he can decide what to do."

"Thomas, huh," Change Tzu said. "Is that best? He has made many bad decisions in the past. What makes you think he can make a good one now?"

"That's beside the point," Haji Abdu said. "He is still the Superintendent of the zoo. It would be rude of us not to visit him. And by the way, you are still refusing to wear your old uniform."

Chang Tzu looked at his robe. "Yes, I have cast aside my former self and you and Betty should too. Take what time you have and search yourself. You may not get another chance."

"Fine," Betty said. "Now give us our shoes."

Chang Tzu slid off Jumbo's back, landing lightly on the ground. He pointed with his flute, "Your shoes are in plain sight, as all things are, on the edge of the fountain."

They went over to the fountain, sat down, and put their shoes on.

"You don't have to play tricks every time we see you," Betty told him.

"Are they tricks—or just another way to look at things?" Chang Tzu asked.

"Seems like a trick to me," Sam said. He liked his shoes and so did Philip. Abby didn't mind. She often thought about going barefoot because her shoe laces always seemed to get in the way.

With their shoes back on, they climbed into their seats on Jumbo and Penny. Chang Tzu watched.

"It was nice to meet you children. But guard yourselves against Thomas. His only concern is himself," Chang Tzu said solemnly. "If you find yourself at odds with him, do not be timid. He is lost and you are not."

Haji Abdu turned Jumbo and Penny out of the courtyard. They waved goodbye to Chang Tzu wondering what his words meant.

They continued their tour until they came to a raised pathway with a sign that read Terrace Walk. The biggest tree they had ever seen towered over everything, engulfing the walkway making it impossible to go further.

The elephants left the walkway and ambled into a pleasant grassy lawn toward the towering tree. Every detail of the tree was gargantuan, in height it was easily several hundred feet tall, primeval and unlike any tree they had ever seen or imagined. Limbs, larger than the biggest of trees, supported massive roots of their own. The trunk, almost as wide as the tree was tall, had rough brown and gray bark that was worn smooth in places and looked like it had been poured out of the sky and cooled into cascades forming the living tree. Perhaps a thousand trees had been molded into this one. They craned their necks looking up at the fantastic tree.

"This is the Great Tree," Haji Abdu said.

"Why is it so big?" Abby asked.

"Not sure," Haji Abdu answered. "You can see how it still grows. The Terrace Walk was passable at one time."

"Why is it called the Great Tree?" Sam asked.

"That's what it has always been called. Your wishes are said to be fulfilled if you ask the tree. It is superstition."

"What kind of tree is it?" Sam asked.

"It's one of a kind," Haji Abdu said. "Maybe the Spanish conquistadors brought it. The town people claimed that the Indians considered this a sacred place, for gathering and ceremony."

The elephants skirted the edge of the tree, weaving in and around the trunk and the tree sized sprawling roots. Once they circumnavigated the tree, they rested.

A crumpled military vehicle, green and rusted, protruded from the mass of roots at the base of the tree. A big jagged drill mounted on the truck was thrust deep into the tree, a failed attempt to conquer the thing. For what reason no one living was left to tell the tale. With time the vehicle would one day be completely gone, consumed by the tree and the strange failure forgotten.

"What happened here?" Philip asked.

"When the military people arrived, they did all sorts of things. They had detailed plans and many rules. To follow orders and rules is not always a bad thing. But the scientists that came with them were another matter." Haji Abdu said. "One in particular was the most thoughtless and driven man I have been unlucky enough to meet. His name was Dr. Cameron Xeno and he was ruthless in his crusade to tear the very idea of life and death from this place. Then one day they just packed up and left. I guess they got what they wanted from the experiments."

"Experiments?" Abby asked, noticing the dark tone of Haji Abdu's words.

"It was an unpleasant time, mostly for the animals. Even poor Jumbo and Penny were subjects." He gently stroked Jumbo's head. "See the suture lines on Jumbo's neck and back? He had his entire skin and organs removed before they put him back together, Penny, too." They stared incredulously at the deep scars on the elephants. "All of the animals had similar things done to them."

Haji Abdu changed the subject, not wanting to remember those dreadful days in the past. He looked skyward and checked the sun's position. "Evening is approaching, and I feel a change in the weather. These old bones can always tell when a storm is on its way," he said, rubbing a bony knee. "Time to move on."

"Why would anyone want to hurt Jumbo and Penny? They're already dead, so what's the point?" Abby asked. She could not understand.

"Abby," Haji Abdu began. "The world can be very cruel, unintentionally, a great deal of the time. The animals that you've seen today are the result of unintentional cruelty. They did not wish to be here, but we desired them and kept them for our own amusement and pride. I myself am not innocent of acting cruel out of ignorance. I have used the bulhook against the elephants during life. They knew fear at my hand. I did not know any better. Now I do and I am at peace with my friends and I believe they forgive me." He paused while old thoughts came and went. "None of the animals here at the zoo survived long, no matter how much care we gave them in the end. But this is a special place and the animals, even though dead, remain as you see them, alive yet not alive. Any living animal or person that has ended its life here cannot truly die. The animals remain to serve their masters and the masters remain to serve them. We are all bound to this place. It is a great mystery. But we have a peace here."

Everyone listened with great interest to his story, even Betty. She nodded her head in agreement.

"Now there are some men in the world that are just plain cruel and crave power. This I believe is why the military men brought the scientists. They wanted to understand death itself, to take it and to serve only them, can you imagine, the hubris to bend death to your will, under the heel of a boot, only to cause harm and punish the world? But as much as they tried they could not take it or understand it. When they realized this, I believe that is why they left. They abandoned us and erased our presence from the outside world until now. You children are the first to discover us since those dark days. And truthfully, it is good to be with the living again," Haji Abdu finished what he had to say. He nudged Jumbo who took his cue and lumbered forward, followed by Penny. Philip, Sam and Abby were silent.

At the edge of the lawn they found another pathway. The elephants trundled along for a while and stopped in front of a neatly kept majestic brick house. Jumbo and Penny each lifted a front leg for them to step down and jump to the ground. Haji Abdu remained seated on Jumbo. Abby hugged Jumbo's leathery face, thanking him for the ride, Sam and Philip shook hands with Penny's nosey trunk.

Haji Abdu said. "I must retire my two large friends for the evening. Betty can introduce you to Thomas. I expect he's expecting you." They watched as the giant elephants and their fierce looking master plodded on and out of sight leaving them stranded in front of a strange house at the end of the day.

⁂ ⁂ ⁂

16

Betty led them up a stone path to the front door of Thomas's house. She banged the brass knocker hanging on the door. They didn't know what to expect from Thomas, this commanding figure, the Superintendent of the zoo, who was both highly thought of and clearly not totally trusted.

Footsteps approached the door. When the door opened, a tall gaunt gray haired man smiled down at them. He wore thin wire glasses and a neat tweed suit, a picture of perfect composure. And he was definitely as dead as the rest of them.

"I've been waiting for you to arrive, Betty. I hope you've taken good care of our guests?" Thomas asked, his pleasant voice sounding formal yet amused.

"We've had a very wonderful day. Abdu and I gave them the grand tour," Betty said.

Thomas politely ignored her and turned his attention to Abby. "And who might you be young lady?"

"Abby Pruitt," she said, shaking his bony hand. He had a half hearted hand shake.

"Pruitt? I believe we had a Pruitt who worked here many years ago."

"That was our grandpa, Archie Pruitt."

"I remember Archie," Thomas said. "What are the odds that members of the Pruitt family would return after all these years? This is most interesting, indeed."

Philip and Sam each introduced themselves, shaking his limp hand.

"Come in, come in, I have something for you that I know you will enjoy."

They entered the house and dumped their backpacks by the door. The cozy living room had a fireplace, some chairs, and an old sofa. The smell of food greeted them reminding them how hungry they were. Thomas noticed. "Yes, I've prepared a meal, not much, but I thought it the proper thing to do for new guests."

A table had been set for them and a black iron pot sat in the corner of the fireplace among the coals. They sat down around the table and Thomas brought the cook pot to them. When he removed the lid the smell of home cooking filled the room.

"Vegetable soup like my mother would make, I think. I can't quite remember what it tasted like, but I believe I used the right ingredients."

They hadn't realized how hungry they were. Since they left TC's house, all they had eaten was junk food. The soup was vegetable and savory but needed something.

"Oh man, where's the salt or pepper or something with flavor?" Sam asked.

"This is all there is," Thomas told him. "Everything in the soup is from my garden. I like to grow turnips and potatoes and such. They always spoil with no one to eat them. But I do enjoy gardening to take my mind off things." He watched with a hint of envy as they finished the meal.

"I can't eat another bite," Abby said. She leaned back in her chair and looked at Thomas.

"You look familiar," she said. "What's your last name?" Thomas looked at her quizzically.

"My last name is Meanwell. I've been Superintendent of the Forest Heights Zoological Park since 1903." he said. "Does that help?"

She sat up abruptly in her chair. "I remember! There's a picture of you in the town library. There's a room full of books that belonged to you."

Thomas looked surprised. Then he started to laugh. "Well, I can't blame her. She never did forgive me for coming back to life."

"Who?" she asked.

"My wife, of course!" Thomas said. "After I died, that was in the winter of 1937, I came back to life. She despised me even more after that. She came from old money, very wealthy, and I was a fool nobody with nothing but a bit of cleverness. She married me anyway and grew bitter. The worlds we came from were so different and I could never reach all the way up to that world. When I died she thought she was finally rid of me. I guess she was in the end. I never heard from her again."

"Oh," Abby replied.

"What's past is past," Thomas said. "I often wish I'd not come back to life. When I think of the pain I caused, it still saddens me. Being dead isn't the best thing that can happen to a person, you know."

"Everyone we've met at the zoo seems to think its okay," Philip said.

A dark look crossed Thomas's face and was gone. "Everyone else is not me." Thomas cleared his throat, "Well, I believe we have plenty of time for stories later. Betty, what do you think? Should we let these young ones have a rest?"

"We've been busy today," Betty replied, wary of the look she had seen come across Thomas' face.

"Then we will let our friends retire to the living room while we clean this mess. How does that sound?" Thomas said.

They agreed. Weariness was creeping up on them.

"Make yourselves at home then. The sofa is especially comfortable," Thomas told them.

In the living room, Philip plopped down onto a stuffed chair and Sam and Abby each took an end of the plush sofa. Slipping off their shoes, they propped up their feet and settled in.

"This is strange," Philip said. "I feel so at home here. Like I don't have a care in the world."

"I feel it, too," Abby said. "I'm not even worried if we ever go back home."

"Let's just stay here. It's more fun anyway," Sam said.

"That sounds nice," Abby said.

"Thomas seems different than the others," Philip said. "I get the feeling he's not as happy being undead."

"He seems a little fake to me," Sam whispered.

Thoughts of staying at the zoo forever rolled around in their heads briefly then soft snoring was the only sound in the room as they took a well deserved nap.

Philip woke first, groggy and with a sore neck from sleeping in the chair. He noticed the light filtering in through the windows was a strange orange color. It reminded him of a day several summers ago when a tornado passed near town. Luckily the mountains kept the tornado away. He heard an ominous rumble in the distance.

He looked at Sam and Abby, still sleeping. He heard another rumble outside and knew a big storm was approaching, just like Haji Abdu predicted. He felt a twinge of nervousness and had the urge to run home.

As he lay in the chair, he heard a metallic jingle. Lifting his head off the armrest, he was surprised to see one of the penguins pull its head out of Abby's backpack with the ring of zoo keys gripped tightly in its beak.

"Hey!" Philip yelled, waking Sam and Abby. He jumped out of his chair.

"Drop those keys, you!" Abby yelled at the penguin, but it was too late. It turned and quickly waddled off down the hall, keys jingling. Abby launched off the couch and chased after the bird.

"That was the one that had me up the tree!" Sam said. "I knew we couldn't trust that beady-eyed little zombie."

Philip tossed Sam his shoes and then slipped his on. He grabbed Abby's shoes and headed down the hall in the direction she had disappeared. She couldn't have gone far. Penguins aren't that fast.

They passed the now silent kitchen. Betty probably went home, and Thomas had disappeared.

"There she is!" Sam said pointing out a window at the back of the house. They watched Abby run barefoot through a garden and out of sight. They found the back door and made their way through the garden. Except for Thomas's carefully tended vegetable patch, everything else, the shrubs and flowers and bushes, was brown and dead.

An eerie orange glow filled the sky. The air was suffocating and not a breeze stirred. They followed a path through the garden and arrived at an old greenhouse: a metal framed structure with a high arched roof completely covered in windows smudged and dirty with age.

Abby sat on a stone bench in front of the decrepit greenhouse, rubbing her foot. Philip dropped her shoes in front of her.

"I followed the little guy here. He ducked into the building where a pane of glass is missing. He sure is quick. He knew exactly where he was going," Abby said. "Now he's gone."

Sam tried the door to the greenhouse. "Locked," he said. "Too bad we don't have the keys."

"Let's try where the penguin went through," Philip said.

They crawled into the building where a pane of glass was missing. They emerged between long rows of tables piled high with all sorts of potted plants. The greenhouse was utterly consumed with plants, it was an indoor jungle. They heard Thomas's voice deep in the green menagerie so they pushed ahead weaving in and out between the rows of tables and plants.

They came to a step leading up to a raised work area. There were tables covered in bottles filled with colorful liquids and laboratory instruments. Scattered around were saplings and cuttings of all sizes taken from the Great Tree. Some had grown quite tall, stretching ominously close to the glass ceiling. Thomas stood in the middle of it all while three familiar penguins waited at his feet. He was admiring the stolen ring of zoo keys.

"Just in time!" Thomas said looking up at the children. "I was worried you would sleep through the night." They could tell he wasn't being sincere, possibly sarcastic.

"I gather you recognize your friends?" Thomas waved a hand toward the three penguins who were preoccupied with grooming themselves. "This is Mino, retriever of my keys, Aiko, and Rambo." Sam snickered.

"Why do you laugh at Rambo?" Thomas asked. "He is a fierce little fellow."

Thomas turned his attention to the ring of keys. "I never gave up looking for these keys. Archie Pruitt and his poor choice of a friend, Warren Goody, wanted to save the zoo. They took my keys planning to come back and undo the damage. So laughable, naive, impossible! You may not realize this but little Mino and Aiko and Rambo have watched you and your family for many years. I was sure the keys would turn up and one day bring you here. " Thomas seemed proud that his forethought and planning had worked.

"What's so great about a bunch of keys?" Philip said. "We used them. They're just for the zoo buildings."

"True. Most of the keys give access to the buildings. But this key in particular is the only one of its kind." Thomas held up a golden key with a tiny tree raised on its surface. "This unlocks a door that few have seen. The military and their scientists would have destroyed this entire town if they had known this key existed."

Thomas leaned in toward them. "Would you like to see what this key is for?" He knew they did. Philip and Sam both nodded yes. Abby stayed silent.

"Then that's settled. This is very exciting. Very exciting indeed!" Thomas said. He put the keys in his jacket pocket, grabbed a vial of amber liquid from a table and put it in another pocket and led them out of the greenhouse. The orange sky had gone and it was dark outside now, the wind howled and lightning flashed as they walked through the dead garden and into his house.

"We must hurry, children! The storm is almost upon us!" Thomas said. He moved quickly through the house, gathering a few things. They grabbed their backpacks from the living room and slung them on. Thomas picked up a lantern and lit it as he headed out the front door.

***

17

Thomas walked fast for a dead guy. His joints creaked and cracked as if he were about to fall apart under his skin. Whatever held him together they didn't want to know.

Philip, Sam, and Abby followed briskly, staying at the edge of the light from Thomas's lantern. The penguins tailed behind not wanting to abandon their master.

The wind gained strength tossing the tree tops and threatened to break them apart. Lightning flashed brightly, throwing strange shadows across their path.

"Are you sure we should be out here?" Abby said. She felt anxious. "I want to go find Betty or Haji Abdu."

"Abby's right," Sam whispered. "I have a bad feeling about this guy. I think he's nuts."

"We have to go with him," Philip said. Sam and Abby looked at him like he was crazy. "Do any of you know how to get back to Betty's place? We would get totally lost. Maybe this won't be so bad."

Thomas left the walkway suddenly and descended into a wooded ravine. They followed a faint trail that ended at a rocky ledge and the entrance of a cave.

When they stopped, the lantern illuminated the rapturous excitement spread across Thomas's face. "We are nearly there, children. You can wait here if you like, but I think you want to see what lies within this cave."

They huddled closer together. No one spoke.

"Very well, follow me," he said.

The cave entrance was tall enough for them to walk under without having to stoop. The air smelled damp and moldy with a hint of crickets and worms. The sound of leaves crunching and rocks scattering under their feet echoed dryly in the dark places of the cave.

Soon the cave narrowed and they had to walk single file and their shoulders brushed against the rough walls. Further on they lost sight of the ceiling high above shrouded in darkness. And there was a chill in the air. The cave had led them into a fracture in the earth. If the ground decided to shift they would be flattened.

Sam, last in line and nearly lost in the dark, bumped into Abby. "Hey!" Sam said. "What's the hold up?"

"I think it's a dead end," Philip said, his voice muffled by the closeness of the walls.

Then there was light as Thomas turned and passed his lantern to Philip.

"Hold this," he said. "And keep it elevated so I can see." Philip held the lantern high and could now see the mass of roots hanging down from high above that blocked their way forward. He watched Thomas reach into his jacket and take out the vial of amber liquid from the greenhouse.

"I perfected this for just such an occasion!" He attached a nozzle to the vial and proceeded to spritz the roots with a fine mist. Shwit, shwit, shwit. "It takes a minute, just wait and see." The liquid was acrid and pungent and it stung their eyes. Nothing happened at first, then a shower of rock and dirt pelted them from the dark void above and the roots quivered and recoiled like tentacles of a giant squid up and out of the way.

Thomas turned back to them, grinning, and took the lantern. "Nothing much but a tincture of vinegar and a few other things. Works like a charm."

The walls widened out, giving them room to spread out, but soon they struggled to find footholds to scramble over bigger and bigger rocks until they had climbed so high in the cave that the way back was lost in darkness. They halted. The cave ended and they were far above the ground in the dark and there was no place left to go.

Thomas held the lantern aloft and found what he was looking for. Indentions had been carved into the cave wall. Each was evenly spaced, gouged into the stone and made for climbing up toward some place. Hand over foot they climbed clinging to each rough niches in the stone for dear life.

When it seemed they could climb no further, they found themselves in a grotto just big enough for all of them to fit in.

"This is great," Sam said. "I knew this wasn't going anywhere."

Clank, clank. The sound of metal being struck. "Hear that?" Thomas asked. "That's the way forward. I know what I'm doing. I'm the only one who does."

Thomas hunched by the light of the lantern. They couldn't see what he was doing. They heard keys jingle as he chose the golden key with the image of a tree, then a lock turned and unlocked. He struggled with something then fell back hard as whatever it was gave way nearly knocking them from their perch.

"It worked!" he said.

A round iron grate had swung open and an opening barely big enough for any of them to get through waited.

Thomas squeezed into the opening and disappeared taking the lantern with him leaving them in receding darkness. They were left alone in this lonely place.

"Oh man, this does not look fun," Abby said. She followed anyway. Sam went in after her and then Philip.

The way was not far and Abby saw light ahead as she crawled. The tunnel became very cramped and narrow. She pulled herself out onto soft grass and fresh air. She lay there catching her breath when Sam and Philip emerged. They had just crawled out of what looked like a rabbit burrow.

Something emanated from this place and they felt it, electricity or gravity or something. It gave them the heebie-jeebies. They didn't know if they could keep going.

A hundred feet or so further in the room, they saw Thomas.

"Come see!" He yelled.

They pushed aside their anxiety and slowly walked toward the light of his lantern. The ground beneath them felt soft and springy under their feet.

"This is grass," Abby said, bending down to feel the ground. "We must be in a field or something. Look!" she said pointing up. Flashes of lightning could be seen high above through shadowy things followed by muffled thunder. Rain dripped down on them.

Thomas stood next to a large pool of water. A few boulders lay on the edge and short grass grew right up to the water. The crystal clear water was only a few feet deep.

"Very pretty, isn't it?" Thomas said, gazing at the water. He held his lantern higher. "Do you see the path within?"

Abby went to one of the boulders and climbed on top to get a better view. "I see something. It looks like a swirl or a spiral," she said. Philip and Sam climbed up the boulder and looked down into the water. Sure enough there was a spiral.

"Weird," Sam said.

At the bottom of the clear pool was a raised spiral of pebbles. The spiral began near the edge of the pool and curved around in tighter and tighter spirals until it reached the center. In the center was a raised circular depression.

"What's that?" Philip said pointing at the spiral center at something bright and colorful moving. "It's a fish!"

"It's guarding something," Abby said.

"Is it gold or treasure?" Sam asked.

"It looks like a rock," Abby said.

"That is no rock young lady," Thomas spoke up. "That, I believe, is the cause of my predicament."

"What do you mean?" Philip asked.

"This is a very old spring," Thomas said. "It's probably been here forever. And it's magic."

"Magic?" Abby said.

"Haven't you noticed? I am dead yet I am not. Every animal, man, and woman that has died at this zoo has remained among the living. If I remove that object from the spring then I believe I can pass on," Thomas began. "I was a terrible Superintendent to the zoo, a miserable husband to my wife in life and in death, and I unthinkingly brought hell upon the zoo, bringing so much pain and suffering."

"It can't be that bad," Abby said, trying to sound supportive.

"It is worse!" Thomas said in anguish. "I invited the military and the scientists to the zoo thinking they would help free us! How could I know they would betray us, torture us, and erase us from history?"

They watched Thomas as his face twisted in torment.

"Where are we?" Philip asked.

"We are inside the Great Tree," Thomas said. "I intend to put an end to my pain tonight."

"That doesn't sound good," Sam whispered.

Thomas set the lantern down at the edge of the spring and waded out into the water. The water came up to his knees. He sloshed and splashed through the water, sending waves in all directions. He disturbed the spiral of pebbles as he went and left a wake of cloudy water. He paid no attention to the mess he created. His only goal was the object in the center.

Thomas stopped at the center of the pool. He sank his arm into the water and grasped the stone object that lay in the eye of the spiral. The colorful fish attempted to fend the intruder off by nipping at Thomas's gnarled hand. The fish would have drawn blood if any still ran through Thomas's veins. Thomas ignored the protective fish.

Thomas brought the object out of the water: A stone figurine carved in the image of a person, maybe a boy, upright and staring forward. It was worn with age, the features smooth as if tumbled in a rushing river.

He turned and waded back to the edge of the spring, the figurine clutched in his hand. As he was about to step out of the water, a look of shock contorted his face. The figurine tumbled from his hand and fell into the grass near the lantern. "Curious," Thomas said before collapsing in the spring, limp and lifeless.

They jumped down from their perch on the boulder and ran over to Thomas.

"I guess he got his wish," Sam said. "He's really dead."

"What do we do now?" Abby asked, sounding frightened. She picked up the figurine. It felt cool and smooth.

"I have a bad feeling about all this," Philip said. He picked up the lantern and held it up to see Thomas, face down, bobbing gently in the water. "Something doesn't feel right."

"I think he's really dead," Abby said.

"Should we pull him out of the water?" Sam asked.

"We can't leave him there. That just seems mean," Abby said. She brushed tears from her cheek. "I've never seen someone die before."

"Well, I'm not sticking one toe in that spring after what just happened! Maybe if we had a stick or something we could..." Philip was saying when Thomas twitched. Philip stumbled backward. Abby screamed.

"That's unnerving," Sam said. "Is he supposed to do that?"

Thomas convulsed violently as if an electric current ran through him. Again and again he convulsed each one harsher than the last. His arms and legs thrashed out, slamming down in the water.

Thomas went still for a moment, and then rose to his feet, water pouring from his clothes. His gaze locked on them. Death burned in his eyes, not cruelty or fear or anger or evil, just death. The Thomas they knew was gone. They knew they were looking at a real zombie. He lurched forward, intent on ending the lives of the three people in front of him.

Abby kept screaming as Thomas came closer. She saw the raw death in Thomas's eyes.

As they turned to escape from Thomas, they saw the Aiko, Mino, and Rambo shambling toward them with the same look of death burning in their eyes. The zombie penguins wanted to kill them.

"Cheese it!" Sam yelled.

Sam ran toward the deadly penguins, jumped over them with room to spare, and ran in the darkness in the direction of where they had entered the clearing inside the tree. Philip and Abby lost sight of him.

Philip, holding the lantern, turned back to face Thomas.

"Aaagh!" Philip yelled as Thomas lurched jerkily at him.

Before Philip could react, Abby ran up to Thomas and kicked him square between his legs. Thomas stumbled back. A look of confusion spread across his face. Abby couldn't help herself, and she cracked a smile.

Sam returned, breathing hard. "I can't find that tunnel! There's no way out of here!" He pulled the machete from its sheath, and he brandished it at Thomas.

Philip felt something hit his leg. He looked down to see the penguins attacking his legs. The penguins slapped his legs mercilessly with their wings. The one called Rambo pecked at his knee cap.

"Ow!" Philip yelled. "That might leave a mark!" He picked up Rambo. "Get lost bird!" he yelled as he flung the penguin off into the darkness. He kicked at Aiko and Mino, looking for the opportunity to fling them, too.

Abby screamed again. Thomas tried to attack Sam, but he was quicker and plunged the machete deep into Thomas's stomach. Thomas landed on Sam, taking him to the ground with his weight. Sam fought to keep Thomas from killing him.

Abby screamed at Thomas, "Why don't you die already!" She threw the figurine as hard as she could at Thomas. The hard stone figurine hit Thomas's head with a loud "thonk!" ricocheted off and landed in the spring. Abby stood there, afraid and angry. Then something happened.

The sound of the figurine splashing in the pond hung in the air. Time stopped. The water in the spring began to swirl, faster and faster. The spiral of pebbles tumbled back into place from the force of the water. The stone figurine rolled back to the center of the spiral, and the fish hovered protectively over it.

There was a loud deep boom that swelled up from deep underground, causing the ground to shake and the tree to tremble. The pool of water settled.

Thomas was gone.

18

Sam lay on his back with the machete pointing into the air where it had moments ago impaled Thomas's gut. He sat up, confused.

Abby looked around expecting to see Thomas coming at her with death in his eyes. Instead, she found the ring of keys Thomas had taken from them. She picked them up and put them in her pocket.

"What do we do now?" Philip yelled, holding Aiko and Mino and Rambo at bay.

"I vote we get out of here," Sam said, standing up. He sheathed his machete. He wasn't about to chop at the penguins. They were still cute, even as zombies.

"We have to climb out of here," Philip said.

Sam took off toward the edge of the tree trunk in search of a way out.

"Where did Thomas go?" Abby said. "He just disappeared."

"That figurine stopped him," Philip said, still kicking at the penguins. "It doesn't matter what happened to him. You saved Sam's life."

Abby thought about this. "I guess I did. Now he owes me."

"Don't count on it!" Sam called out from the darkness.

"It's sad really. Thomas wanted to end what happened to him, but he made things worse," Abby said. "Do you think all the animals are zombies? What about Betty and Haji Abdu and Chang Tzu?"

"I think they're all zombies," Philip said, getting annoyed with the penguins.

"I wonder why the animals didn't disappear, too," Abby said.

"Hey guys! This is it!" Sam yelled, climbing.

"Should we leave the penguins?" Abby said.

"What choice do we have? It's either them or us, and I like us better right now," Philip said.

They ran toward the sound of Sam's voice. They left the penguins by the side of the spring. Thomas's lantern, still sitting on the grass, flickered and went out.

Philip and Abby climbed up the inside of the tree toward Sam, positive this was the tree they had seen when they rode Jumbo and Penny earlier that day. The hanging roots and intertwining limbs, covered with thick smooth bark, made climbing easy. Philip got the headlamp out of his backpack and turned it on. The nooks and hollow inside the tree would be great to explore. Someday! But now they had to survive.

Climbing higher inside the tree, the bark became wet and slippery. Heavy rain fell outside. They soon found an opening big enough to climb into and pushed and shoved their way through limbs and roots into a shelter big enough for them to rest in, protected from the full force of the torrential downpour outside.

"Can you see anything?" Philip yelled over the incessant din of rain.

Sam leaned to the edge of the tree. "I can't even see the ground! We're stuck!"

Finding a quiet, dry corner in the tree shelter, they settled in for the rest of the night.

"Let's wait it out," Philip suggested. "If we try to climb down now in the rain, we could fall. It'll be safer in the morning."

"I can't believe they're all zombies," Abby said. "The animals. The people. They *all* want to attack us like Thomas and the penguins did."

"Yep," Philip said. The thought of fighting their way through the zoo filled him with dread.

"I liked Betty," Abby mumbled.

"Maybe it won't be so bad," Sam said. "We got away from those penguins and Thomas just disappeared. Where did he go anyway?"

"Maybe he went to the moon," Philip said. "He was going to kill us. Does it matter where he went?"

"I wanted him gone. Obliterated. Dead. I was so scared when he was attacking you Sam," Abby said. "I think I wished him away."

"You definitely did the right thing," Philip said. "Anyway, you did what he couldn't do. He's gone. Just like he wanted."

"I hope we can get home," Abby said.

"We'll wait till morning," Philip said. "First we've got to get out of this tree. Then we'll figure a way out of the zoo." He tried to reassure himself

"There are hundreds of zombie animals out there, killer zombie lions and blood-thirsty pandas. They all want to get us," Sam worried.

Lightning flashed and a crash of thunder silenced them.

"Okay then. Who wants a snack?" Philip asked, changing the subject and attempting to sound cheerful.

They ate what was left of their food before settling into a secure spot against the tree and after a while they fell into a deep, dreamless sleep.

***

19

"Bright!" Philip said, shielding his eyes from the morning sun. The rain stopped sometime during the night and now the sky was bright blue and cloudless, and the summer heat had been swept after the storm. As Philip looked down from his perch high in the impossibly giant Great Tree, a nice breeze ruffled his sandy hair. The zoo was flooded. Water was everywhere. The higher grounds of the zoo were islands separated by the flooded walkways. The base of the tree was encircled by water and the Terrace Walk far below was barely visible. The storm had wreaked havoc upon the zoo. Trees were knocked down and lay scattered.

"Holy cow!" Sam said rubbing the sleep out of his eyes. "I'm glad we stayed up here last night."

"Look how high we are," Abby said stretching her sore muscles. "How do we get down?"

They were only about half way up the towering tree and they could not see the top because of the canopy of tangled roots and giant limbs stretching in every direction.

"We'll just climb down the same way we climbed up," Philip said. "Only this time, we'll climb on the outside of the tree and not the inside."

"And then what?" Sam asked.

"We'll find Betty," Abby said.

"What?" Sam said. "She's a zombie and she would kill us now if she saw us!"

"Quit!" Philip interrupted. "Sam's right, Abby. Betty's most likely a zombie now. We've got to be careful if we want to make it out of here alive."

Sam and Abby stopped bickering.

"Let's climb down," Philip said.

Abby pointed at a rooftop among the trees and water across the zoo. "That's Betty's building!"

Sam rolled his eyes at Abby.

They shouldered their backpacks once again and started the climb down the tree. Soon they forgot their worries and they began to have fun walking along the branches and sliding down the smooth hanging roots to each lower branch, and then sliding down another and so on. It was easy! Close to the base of the tree, they walked out along a giant limb and lowered themselves onto the arched Terrace Walk, which barely stuck out from the water all around.

They stood on the submerged bridge, wondering what to do. Dirty brown water surrounded them. It appeared the only way across to dry land was to swim.

"We need a boat," Sam said.

"Good luck with that," Philip replied.

"What about that? Could that work?" Abby pointed toward something floating next to the Great Tree.

"That's perfect!" Philip exclaimed. Bobbing in the water was a big white swan, its body cracked and faded and covered with grim. It had a bench seat on its back and bicycle-like foot peddles that turned a paddle wheel in the rear.

"It must have washed in," Philip said. "When we crossed that bridge over the pond the other day it said something about paddle-boat rides."

"Somebody go get it!" Abby said, looking at her brothers.

"I'll do it," Sam said. "I'm still wet from last night."

Sam waded into the water and swam out to the paddle boat. He climbed aboard, sat down and began paddling. But instead of moving forward, the paddle boat turned in circles. Philip and Abby laughed.

"Go and help him," Abby said.

"Why me?" Philip asked.

"'Cause I'm your sister," Abby replied as if that was enough explanation.

Philip didn't want to argue. He swam out to Sam and climbed into the other seat and began paddling. Once they had the paddle boat pointed in the right direction, they paddled in unison, splashing clumsily up to the Terrace Walk to get Abby.

"This thing can move pretty good once you get the hang of it," Sam said, breathing hard from the workout.

"It's kind of noisy don't you think?" Abby said. "All that splashing is going to attract attention."

"We'll paddle quietly," Philip said. Abby climbed on and squeezed in between them.

"Aye, aye, Captain," Sam said, giving a salute.

They turned the paddle boat toward deeper water. No matter how carefully they paddled, the wheel splashed noisily in the water.

"The longer we stay in the water, the better," Philip said. "If this paddleboat washed out of the scenic pond that cuts through the zoo then we don't have to walk."

"If we stay off the land we can avoid the animals and any of the people wandering around," Abby said, confirming his logic, trying to stay positive.

"Zombies you mean. Avoid the zombies," Sam said.

They paddled along at a determined leisurely pace. The water became deeper once they entered the Scenic Loop Pond. They steered into the middle of the deep pond making sure to stay away from the shore.

"Oh, no!" Abby said.

"What?" Philip asked. They stopped paddling and drifted in the open water. Without the constant splashing, they could hear the zoo and the unnatural animal calls.

"Look!" Abby yelled. She pointed at the shore line on their right where a crowd of animals had gathered: zebras, monkeys, rhinoceroses, peacocks, chimpanzees, snakes, hamsters, gerbils. The animals sensed them and gravitated to them. The zombies were drawn to the only living things in the zoo and they had only one all consuming purpose left, to extinguish the lives of the three children floating in the paddleboat listing toward shore. The zombie animals launched forward into the water flailing and splashing, horrifying sounds growled from their throats.

Philip and Sam paddled with all their might spinning in a circle. The paddle wheel spun fast churning up a wide wake behind them attracting more zombies.

Haji Abdu waved at them from the bridge just ahead. That meant they were close to the front gate and a way out. "Hurry!" he yelled. He didn't seem to be a murderous zombie so they paddled furiously toward him.

Bump. The paddleboat hit something under the water.

"Did you feel that?" Sam asked, forgetting to paddle.

"We must have hit a log!" Philip said, letting his feet off the pedals. Bubbles surfacing all around the boat.

"Whoa! What's that smell?" Abby said.

Bump. The paddleboat rocked again.

"Paddle! Paddle!" Philip yelled at Sam as they headed toward the shore.

Directly in their path a smelly hippopotamus, grisly and bloated, surfaced. It was too late to stop, and they paddled over the top of it, nearly capsizing the paddleboat.

"Go, Go, Go!" Sam yelled, slamming the paddleboat into the hard bank. They jumped out just as the zombie hippopotamus attacked the paddleboat made to look like a serene white swan, crushing it with its enormous jaws, and dragging it down into the murky depths.

The children sprinted to Haji Abdu.

"I'm so relieved to find you three. I feared the worst," Haji Abdu said. "Come on, we've no time to waste!" The zombie animals on this side of the pond felt their presence and lumbered up the walkway toward them. Haji Abdu quickly led them to the building Betty lived in.

"How did you know we were headed this way?" Abby asked.

"I didn't," Haji Abdu said. "I just hoped you would."

Philip tried the door handle. "It's locked, of course! Where are the keys?"

"I have them. I have them," Abby said. "I picked them up." She took her backpack off and rummaged around. "Oh, no! I can't find them."

"We don't have time for this!" Sam yelled.

They heard a deep growl and saw a mangy zombie lion and her cubs striding toward them.

Sam started beating on the door. "Let us in, Betty! Betty!"

"Here they are! I found them!" Abby said, pulling the keys from her pants pocket. She quickly picked a key and unlocked the door. They piled into the lobby, slamming the door shut behind them just as the pride of lions arrived. The lions scratched and growled at the door determined to get to their prey. A crowd of animals quickly crowded outside the building. The children were trapped inside. Betty was hiding behind the reception desk looking very distraught.

"My friends," she said.

"Are you okay?" Abby asked as she hugged Betty. "We were worried you turned into a zombie."

"Something happened to me last night, but I feel better now," Betty smiled. "I must have lost my wits because I can't remember anything. I woke up this morning with my home all in a mess." The place did look messy. Chairs and tables were overturned. Things were scattered across the floor.

"Thomas turned everyone and every animal into zombies," Abby told her.

They told Betty and Haji Abdu about their experience the previous night: how Thomas took them into the Great Tree; how he wanted to end it all; about the spring and the figurine; how he turned into a zombie and attacked them; and how Abby saved them.

"So Thomas is dead," Haji Abdu said.

"We think so," Philip said. "He's gone."

"By putting the figurine back in the spring, you saved us from a fate worse than death," Haji Abdu said. "You did us a great service. We owe you our lives."

This made them feel a lot better, especially Abby.

"But it's troubling that the animals are still affected," Haji Abdu said. "We can only hope the change wears off so we can continue our peaceful existence. Time will tell."

"Can you help us find a way out of the zoo so we can go home?" Abby asked. "We were going to try the front gate."

"That is the surest way," Haji Abdu said. "It's not far. But with the animals out to find you, we will have to be very careful."

* * *

20

It looked like all the zombie zoo animals had gathered outside the office building, growling and drooling and terrible. They were drawn to the children and the life they possessed, and to the undead adults as well, perhaps for their closeness to the living. Nothing could stop the zombie animals from their prey until all life was driven from the zoo.

No one dared look outside and risk bringing more attention. Instead, Haji Abdu and Betty led them down a flight of stairs into the basement of the building. Haji Abdu knew many things about the zoo, and he had a plan. It began in the basement.

Betty held a lamp that lit the darkness. Chairs, file cabinets, junk, and cardboard boxes stuffed with papers filled the cavernous basement. The maze of forgotten furniture and supplies were covered in dust and cobwebs.

"I haven't been down here in years," Betty said, disgusted by the layers of dust.

Haji Abdu weaved through the maze and stopped at a long wooden crate with metal latches. The words "Cockle Mk II" were stenciled in black across it. He undid the latches that sealed the box and flipped the lid open. A neatly stacked pile of wooden slats, several short paddles, and a folded bluish gray mass of rubberized canvas were inside. The underside of the lid had an instruction diagram: It was for a collapsible military kayak.

"First thing we need to do is assemble this boat," Haji Abdu said. "These were used during wartime. We will put it to better use."

While Betty held the lamp, they all went to work assembling the frame and all the pieces. The rubberized canvas cover had stiffened and was difficult to pull over the frame, but when they finished they had a fine looking kayak with a cockpit big enough for Philip, Sam, and Abby to squeeze into.

Haji Abdu found a coiled length of rope and tossed it into the cockpit along with two short paddles. He grabbed a loop of rope at the front, Philip took hold of a loop at the rear, and they lifted the boat and carried it to a wide door at the end of the basement and set it down. He slid the heavy door to one side, its metal rollers squealed. A dark corridor lay beyond.

"The tunnel leads east to the old train terminal here at the zoo. Maintenance crews would use this corridor to move supplies back and forth, the military, too," Haji Abdu said. "The animals crowding the zoo above won't know we passed them by."

Betty handed the lamp to Sam. "This is far as I go," she said. "You don't need my help to get where you are going."

"Thanks, Betty. It was nice meeting you," Philip said, shaking her hand goodbye.

"If you're ever in our neighborhood don't be a stranger," Sam said. "I really liked meeting you, too. You're a pretty neat old lady, being dead and all."

Abby hugged Betty. "I'll miss you," Abby said, tears dampened her cheeks.

"Don't cry, Abby," Betty told her. "It's only goodbye. I know we'll meet again. It's not like I'm going anywhere."

Abby nodded and let go.

Haji Abdu and Philip lifted the kayak again and went into the corridor. Sam followed with the lamp with Abby dragging behind. They waved goodbye to Betty as she slid the door shut with a squeal of rusty rollers and a loud clang. The sound echoed down the tunnel.

The corridor was wide enough for Sam and Abby to walk on either side of the kayak. The rock-lined walls supported an arched ceiling. Water dripped into thin puddles on the floor.

After several minutes of walking they came to a set of doors. Sam and Abby pressed the release bar on each door and shoved them open so Haji Abdu and Philip could carry the kayak through. Daylight greeted them, and Sam extinguished the lamp and set it by the doors.

They walked up a wide service ramp and came out through a loading area in the train terminal complex. The main terminal building was similar to the depot downtown, but this one was much bigger and more ornate, red brick, lots of windows, ironwork, and the railroad line ran along the far side. The old train engine sat there like a slumbering giant, ready to be awakened. Several passenger cars and a caboose were still attached to it. There were side tracks so the train could turn around and go back and forth to town.

They carried the kayak by the ticket booths with the tri-pronged counter machines that people used to pass through. Once beyond the terminal complex, they could see down the Grand Way where a crowd of zombie animals had gathered in front of the building they had just escaped. It was certain that if Haji Abdu had not found them, they would have been trapped in that building forever—or until the zombie animals forced their way in.

The last length of the Grand Way led up to a large wrought iron gate and an immense stone wall that stretched in either direction and out of sight, enclosing the zoo. Above the entrance, in massive black iron, read FOREST HEIGHTS ZOOLOGICAL PARK. They set the kayak down. Haji Abdu went to the gate, turned a handle, and lifted a heavy metal bar out of the groove in the ground that held it in place. He pushed one half of the gate open just enough for them to pass through.

"I thought the gate was sealed," Philip said.

"It was. I'll show you."

He closed the gate behind them so no animal could follow. Haji Abdu lifted a metal sign that lay face down in the leaves. It read, "Contaminated Area, No Trespassing, Lethal Force Will Be Used Against Violators." He let the sign drop back into the leaves.

They continued on through what used to be a parking area. Trees had grown up through the paving where families once parked their cars on their visits to the zoo. No families would park here ever again. Nature had nearly completed its task of taking the land back. A trace of road led them to the edge of a bluff that skirted most of the zoo. Below them, Crooked Creek ran its course. The remains of a bridge foundation clung to the rock, and its twin on the opposing bluff stood in ruin.

Haji Abdu retrieved the coil of rope, unwound it, and tied an end to the loop handle on the front of the kayak. Philip, Sam, and Abby stuffed their backpacks into the boat.

"I wish you to make it home safely," Haji Abdu said. "I am pleased to have met you."

"Will everything at the zoo go back to normal?" Abby asked.

"In time, I'm sure," he replied. "All things return to a balance given enough time."

Haji Abdu secured the rope against a tree and lowered the kayak over the side of the bluff. He let it hang in the air, swinging just above the surface of the water.

Philip and Sam each shook Haji Abdu's hand, and Abby could not resist giving him a hug. They stepped up to the edge of the bluff. Philip, not keen on high places, jumped first. He whooped on the way down, splashing into the deep pool that ran along the base of the bluff. Sam held Abby's hand as they jumped, yelling for the fun of it.

Haji Abdu lowered the kayak into the water. Philip untied the rope from the boat and Haji Abdu pulled it back up. The children swam the boat to a gravel bar on the opposite bank, pushed their backpacks as far into the bulkhead as they could and climber into the cockpit: Sam in front; Philip in back, and Abby squeezed in the middle. Philip and Sam each took one of the short paddles.

They looked up at Haji Abdu and waved. He called down to them, "Until we meet again!" They pushed off from the gravel bar and the current pulled them along. He watched them descend into a series of rapids and disappear around the bend. He turned and went home.

***

21

Crooked Creek was up. The rain during the night had raised the water just enough to make their trip fun. While Philip tried to steer the kayak and Sam paddled, Abby surveyed the scenery. They paddled into every wave and rapid they came to. The bigger rapids sent water over the front of the boat, spraying them. They plowed through the rapids for several miles, having fun and cheering and laughing all the way.

They passed the bluff shelter where their adventure had begun at the beginning of summer. They barely noticed it as they dodged boulders and ran rapids.

The water flattened out, and they paddled hard on the last stretch to the low-water bridge they had crossed two days earlier on their bikes. They eased up to the bank before getting to the bridge. The creek was spilling over the concrete slab of a bridge and water swirled fiercely around the large pipes that went under it. They didn't want to get sucked into those pipes. They got out onto the bank and pulled the kayak out of the water, securing it in the weeds near the road. They walked down the road to where they had hidden their bikes and rode quickly back to the bridge. Philip and Sam managed to balance the kayak on the handlebars of their bikes and they pushed their bikes over the low water bridge. The water was swift and up to their ankles but they made it across. They crossed Highway 7, followed the sidewalk and took the next street bringing them again past the driveway leading to the Pig Lady's strange home.

As they rolled past her driveway, they were very surprised to see Pastor Newton collecting the Sunday paper. He glared at the kids pushing the kayak quickly along.

Abby stared right back at him and said, "Betty says, Hi!"

Pastor Newton dropped his paper. His face twitched and reddened. He stared off into space, forgetting about the kids passing by. He stood there until they were long gone. But he got the message.

They pushed their bikes up a few more streets and over a hill before arriving home. They rolled the kayak up to the basement doors where Mr. Pruitt was busy working on something and parked their bikes. They lifted the kayak off the handlebars and sat it next to the house and left their bikes in the driveway.

Mr. Pruitt was glad to see his children. "Where did you get the kayak?

It's a beauty."

"A friend gave it to us," Abby said.

"Well," Mr. Pruitt said. "You can tell me the story over dinner."

They walked through the basement and headed up the stairs to the kitchen where they heard familiar music playing.

"What's for dinner?" Sam asked. "We're starving."

"Pizza," Mr. Pruitt said.

The magic word: pizza! Philip, Sam, and Abby knew the world was right again. They opened the door to the kitchen, went inside, closed the door behind them, and enjoyed the perfect end to a very long adventure. Well, perfect for a little while, anyway.

***

22

Summer vacation ended and they were back in school. Routine and homework was the norm again. One autumn afternoon, Philip watched as Abby traced her finger along the front glass of the big aquarium in his room. The large colorful fish in the tank followed her finger closely. The fish probably thought her finger was a worm or a bug. Fish aren't really known for their intelligence. They were having a good time when Sam burst into Philip's room and quickly shut the door behind him. He carried his backpack and his baseball glove. He looked very excited.

"You aren't going to believe this!" Sam said barely getting the words out quick enough.

"What? You found someone who will play catch with you," Abby said turning her attention to her brother, leaving the fish wondering where the worm disappeared to.

Sam ignored her comment. He put the baseball glove on, opened the dirty backpack, and reached in with the glove. He pulled his hand out, gripping something tightly in the wide fold of the leather.

"It's been what, three months since we went to that crazy undead zombie zoo?" Sam said. Philip and Abby nodded.

"I was cleaning my room...," Sam began when Philip cut him off. "You were cleaning your room?"

"Ok. I was pushing everything under the bed. Happy?" Sam answered.

"You may continue," "Philip replied trying to annoy him.

"I found my backpack that I took with me on our trip. I thought there might be some candy left over, so I figured it was still good and I would eat it. When I opened the bag it was all torn wrappers and chocolate and peanuts. Everything was ripped up. When I dumped the bag out in the trash I found this." Sam carefully opened his glove and showed them what had gotten him so excited.

A small furry gerbil sat on its haunches in the middle of the baseball glove. It held its little paws out in front of it as if it was ready to grab hold of the nearest living thing. Its long whiskers twitched as it smelled its captors. Its black beady eyes could only see death.

"He's a stowaway from the zoo. He's been in my backpack all this time," Sam said.

"Oh look he's so adorable!" Abby cooed as she reached to pick it up.

"No, Abby!" Philip and Sam both warned.

Abby stopped in mid-reach but the zombie gerbil had other plans. It leapt horribly fast at Abby's face. It landed on her head and she twirled around trying to get it out of her hair. She flung the gerbil off and it landed in the big aquarium.

The fish spotted the gerbil and decided to investigate. Perhaps it thought this was dinner or another friendly fish. The zombie gerbil saw the fish and it did what all zombie gerbils do. It attacked. It latched onto the fish with its dangerous little claws and sunk its sharp teeth into the fish's flesh. The fish new something was wrong and it swam frantically around the tank trying to get rid of the furry monster.

Within moments it was over. The poor fish sunk to the bottom of the tank with the gerbil still clinging to its back. The fish was no more. With this life ended the gerbil released its grip and drifted to the front of the aquarium. It could see the kids staring at it from the room. The look of horror on their faces did not register in the gerbil's brain. It clawed at the glass trying to get at them.

"No! Fishy!" Abby yelled.

"Well, I didn't expect that to happen," Sam said remorsefully.

"I had Fishy for two years Sam!" Philip yelled. "You could have just told us about the gerbil."

"You think the fish will come back to life like in the movies?" Sam asked, distraught.

"It doesn't look like it," Philip said. "This isn't a movie you know."

"I know. But in the movies anytime a zombie bites someone they turn into one too," Sam said.

"Yeah well, Fishy looks pretty dead. He's not even twitching," Philip said.

Abby had an idea. "You know what this means? Those animals at the zoo are still zombiefied! They never changed back!" She looked worried.

"Betty and Haji Abdu and Chang Tzu are probably trapped or worse," she said. "We're going to have to go back and help."

"How would we help? Storm in and get ourselves killed. Remember all those zombie animals wandering around? Lions, remember the lions?" Sam said.

"For starters let's get that gerbil out of the aquarium before mom or dad sees it," Philip said.

Philip grabbed a net and fished the little monster out of the water. With its fur all wet it looked like a hairball a cat coughed up, a hairball with dark beady eyes full of death.

"We need to put him in something," Abby said.

"Got it!" Sam left the room in a hurry.

He came back carrying an elaborate castle with a drawbridge and windows constructed of multi-colored Legos. He put it on a table for them to admire.

"Ta da!" Sam said proudly.

"It's a sweet castle but how will it help?" Philip asked.

"I built it earlier for the gerbil. It even has a dungeon," Sam explained pushing aside the top of the castle tower to reveal a tiny enclosure.

"This should hold him. And he can even look out through the windows so he won't get lonely," Sam added.

"Why didn't you just bring him in like this? It would have saved Fishy," Philip asked trying to understand his brother's logic.

"I'm a showman at heart. It's all about presentation," Sam explained. "I figured it would be more exciting to bring the little guy in the way I found him and not all cramped in his little dungeon."

"That makes sense," Abby teased. "Endanger us all. You want me to go get the cat and introduce him too?"

"Abby," Philip interrupted. "Go get your hair dryer. And maybe some perfume. If we stick him in the dungeon like this he's going to start stinking worse."

After a minute under the hair dryer and a spray of perfume the deadly gerbil looked good. He could pass for living they thought.

A knock at the door startled them.

"Coming in kids," Mr. Pruitt came in the room before they could hide the tiny rodent.

"What have you got there?" Mr. Pruitt asked, craning to get a better look.

No one knew what to say. Should they tell their dad that they have a zombie gerbil that kills anything it sees?

"You have to take that back from wherever you got it," Dad told them. "Your mother really doesn't like rats."

"It's not a rat. It's a gerbil," Abby corrected. "And he's just visiting."

"Oh, just visiting, huh? In that case, as long as you keep him out of your mother's sight it should be okay," Mr. Pruitt said. "Does our guest have a name?" He reached his hand toward the gerbil.

The gerbil saw the hand coming and his little mouth gaped, ready to chomp down on some living flesh. Mr. Pruitt noticed and pulled his hand back. "He looks like a biter."

"His name is Steve," Abby said. The name just popped in her head. "Steve Gerbil."

"He sounds important, like an executive or a businessman," Mr. Pruitt said. "Anyway, just keep him out of sight." Mr. Pruitt left the room and then stepped back in.

"Oh yeah, the reason I came in here in the first place was to see who wanted to go get an ice cream in a little bit?" Mr. Pruitt said.

"Come downstairs to the basement when you're ready." He left the room again.

"Okay," they said in unison.

"That was close," Philip said. "What kind of name is Steve Gerbil, Abby?"

Abby smiled, "I have no idea. He just kind of looks like a Steve."

Sam used his baseball glove making sure not to expose any flesh near the gerbil's sharp teeth and put the fur ball of death into the castle dungeon.

From a narrow window in the dungeon, they could see light glint off of Steve's beady eyes.

"Are you sure this will hold him?" Philip asked Sam, concerned.

"You kidding? Those walls are three blocks thick," Sam said expertly. "It's an engineering marvel. A squirrel might bust through but not a gerbil. It's got buttresses. See the buttresses?"

"I'm looking at a buttress right now," Philip said giving Sam a look.

"Who's going to keep him?" Abby asked.

"Looks like you will since you named him," Philip told her. "Just don't let him out."

Abby seemed pleased with this idea. She liked animals, even this poor zombie gerbil.

"What should we do about the zoo?" Abby wondered.

"I don't know. If Steve Gerbil is a zombie, then all the other animals are too," Philip said.

"We'll figure something out," Sam said trying to be encouraging. "First, ice cream, then, adventure."

❊❊❊

Part II

23

It was a warm, sunny day. In fact, it was just too nice a day to be the first weekend of December. It felt like a spring day. If it wasn't for the bare leafless trees, one would never guess winter was near. The Pruitt family was out and about on this lovely day. This was a tradition, of sorts. On the first weekend of December they would pile into the rusty blue and white Land Cruiser wagon, and go in search of a Christmas tree.

Typically, on this weekend, it was cold and they would be bundled up in heavy coats with the Land Cruiser's heater cranked up all the way, which didn't help much since it would only blast air a few degrees warmer than the outside air, and it sometimes smelled like exhaust. Today, the windows were rolled down and the breeze stirred up dust in the cab of the truck.

There was no telling where they would get a Christmas tree. Mr. Pruitt would find a different spot each year without fail. One year, after driving all day, he parked on the side of the road and cut down a tree from an overgrown fence line. Then, another year, he just took a tree out of the back yard. This year, they got a surprise when the old Land Cruiser turned off the road and bounced over the low water bridge that spanned Crooked Creek.

Since discovering the zombie gerbil in Sam's backpack last week, they talked endlessly about what to do to help their friends at the zoo. But they could never come up with a plan. School kept them busy enough and now the non-stop barrage of the Christmas season was distracting them.

Now, memories of the zoo flooded back to them. Thoughts of wise Haji Abdu, kind Betty Goody, and aloof Chang Tzu, trapped by the animals twisted into terrible zombies, worried them. Philip,

Sam, and Abby were the only people alive that knew of the desperate situation at the forgotten zoo of the undead.

"Dad? Where are we going?" Philip asked.

"I got a tip that there's a Christmas tree farm down this way," Mr. Pruitt said with confidence.

They continued on for a few miles until the road ended. A narrow, deeply rutted trail disappeared in the woods in front of them. "This can't be," Mr. Pruitt mumbled to himself. "I didn't see any other turnoffs."

"Philip, hop out and lock the hubs! That tree farm has to be around here somewhere." Philip jumped out. He went to the front of the truck, and with all the strength in his fingers he turned the mechanism at the center of each front tire to the locked position.

"Honey, let's turn around and get a tree from the lot downtown," Mrs. Pruitt said. She was not in the mood to go four-wheeling through the woods. "You know how you get. We'll be out here all day driving in circles, and then you'll get mad."

Philip got back in the truck, banged the door shut, and then Mr. Pruitt downshifted into low four-wheel drive. There was a loud grinding as gears locked into place. The Land Cruiser gave a jerk forward and everyone was thrown back into their seats. The truck lurched into the woods and crawled along the rutted trail. The Land Cruiser was unstoppable.

Weaving through the big trees, branches, and any small trees that got in the way, it all scraped loudly against the panels and undercarriage of the truck. This was not a big deal. Mr. Pruitt had done this many times before. A few more dings and scratches on the truck didn't bother him. They pushed forward, straddling the deep ruts and navigating over boulders. Soon the trail looked impassable. It zigzagged up and over a steep hill before them. "Hold on," Mr. Pruitt said with a big smile.

The Land Cruiser inched up the hill, wheels spinning as loose gravel gave way under the tires. The motor roared and the transmission threatened to jump out of gear. Mrs. Pruitt gripped the safety handle on the dash in front of her. Philip and Sam held onto the doors, and Abby, who sat in the middle, braced herself against the front seats, trying not to get bounced onto the floor.

"This doesn't seem like a good idea!" Mrs. Pruitt said, sounding shrill.

"Don't worry! I think I know where we are!" Mr. Pruitt said, having a great time.

They went over a brute of a boulder, and the back end of the truck hit the rock with a loud, bone-jarring bang that shocked them all. The Land Cruiser sputtered and died.

"It's okay," Mr. Pruitt said, still in a good mood. "Just bogged her down." He turned the key and the truck started back up. He threw it into gear, and the truck bucked and went on.

At the top of the hill, they had a panoramic view of the forest below. The leaves had fallen from the trees—except for one. Across the valley, Philip saw the green top of a very large tree that rose above the forest. It was the Great Tree, the great primordial tree that protected a spring with a little stone figurine in its crystal waters, at the center of the zoo. He nudged Abby and pointed toward the tree. Sam noticed, too. Mr. and Mrs. Pruitt didn't seem to be aware of it.

"There it is!" Mr. Pruitt said confidently. He pointed down in the valley at a dirt road. A few cars drove along the road to a large pasture where other cars were parked.

Mr. Pruitt followed the trail down the far side of the steep, stomach-churning hill, over a fallen tree that blocked the trail and more boulders. After a few tense moments, the Land Cruiser pulled onto the dirt road. "See, I knew this was a shortcut," Mr. Pruitt said.

They followed the proper dirt road to a parking area at the edge of a pasture, and Mr. Pruitt parked the truck with the other vehicles. Quite a few people must have gotten the tip about the tree farm. Even their neighbors were here. Word of a bargain spread quickly.

The grove of Christmas trees stood together in the pasture at the edge of the forest beyond. A Quonset hut looking like a giant soup can half-buried in the ground, its corrugated steel roof brown with rust, was nearly hidden across the pasture, beyond the stand of trees. There was a nice old farm house nearby, a few outbuildings, and farm equipment.

The Pruitt family clambered out of the Land Cruiser and joined the gathered crowd busy choosing Christmas trees.

"How you folks doin'?" A spry very old man dressed in worn blue coveralls and a flannel shirt came up and shook hands with Mr. and Mrs. Pruitt. "Stan Barr is the name," he said, his quick eyes not missing a thing.

"Fine, fine. Can you believe this weather? Doesn't quite feel like the holidays," Mr. Pruitt said.

"Makes me feel young again," Stan said honestly. "Snow will be here soon enough. I remember a warm spell like this, way back when I was young. We got near two foot of snow for Christmas. It was warm just like this."

While Mr. Pruitt and Stan talked earnestly back and forth about the weather, Mrs. Pruitt led the kids into the grove of Christmas trees. Mrs. Pruitt never could understand why grown men obsessed about the weather.

They mingled among the trees with the other families. The aroma of evergreen and pasture was pleasant. Mrs. Pruitt found a group of ladies she knew and was soon preoccupied. They wandered off and quickly found a group of children playing hide and seek among the Christmas trees.

Abby was picked as "it" and had to count to twenty with her eyes closed before she could go find someone else. She was the only girl, so, of course, she "it".

She counted out loud. "Eighteen, nineteen, and twenty, ready or not, here I come!" she yelled, letting the other kids know she was out to find them. She opened her eyes. No one was around. She could hear the adults talking in another row of trees. She knelt down hoping to catch a glimpse of someone's shoe under one of the trees, but no luck. She headed off away from the sound of the voices where the trees were close together.

She crept along weaving in and out around the trees until she came to the edge of the grove. The silent Quonset hut was just beyond the trees. A door was open that led into the half-moon front of the building. She saw someone move and the door slowly close. "That has to be Sam in there," she thought. "Only he would go where he didn't belong."

She ran over to the door, opened it wide, and looked in. It was dark inside and she couldn't see anything. She flipped the light switch next to the door and the place lit up. It was much larger inside than it looked from the outside.

It was filled with all kinds of stuff: big mechanical things, tool benches, machines, tires, and shelves of boxes and cans. It was tidy and organized, and it was obvious someone was busy tinkering and maintaining all of this.

"Sam! Are you in here?" Abby called out into the room. No answer. "You aren't supposed to be in here, you dummy!" she said uncertainly. She walked further into the building looking under benches and bulky machines and then she stopped. At the back of the building was the coolest vehicle she had ever seen. It was huge. It was dark green with a bright white star on the side, a military vehicle, and it looked like a big boat with wheels.

"Whoa!" she said. "What is that?"

"That's my duck," said someone behind her in a drawling, extra-Southern, comically cornball, Southern accent.

Abby turned and nearly fell down she was so startled. Standing in front of her was a man dressed in green coveralls with the name Barr stitched over a front pocket. He didn't seem threatening in any way. Actually, he looked rather pleased to be talking to someone. He had a big grin on his face and a tightly parted head of short dark hair greased flat and shiny. He waited for Abby to reply.

Abby had a hard time getting her thoughts together. Although this person was friendly enough, there was one big, glaring thing wrong with him. Abby had seen this problem before.

"You're not alive are you?" Abby asked boldly. She was not bothered by the fact. Unless, of course, he was a zombie and wanted to destroy her.

"Hot diggitty dog! How'd you know that? I can't remember anyone ever asking me that!" the man said in that funny drawl, genuinely pleased with Abby's straight-forward manner.

"Well, you just don't look alive," Abby told him. "You don't look as shriveled and dried out as the others. You look better, fresher maybe."

"Others?" the man asked. He looked very interested.

"Like the others at the zoo," Abby replied. "You've got to be from the zoo too."

The man's jaw dropped in wonder. He sat down on a chair. "Wonders never cease," he said.

"My name is Private Frank Ulysses Barr, and you must be Nancy Drew 'cause I never met someone so smart." He held out his hand to her.

She shook his hand and laughed at his joke. His hand was cold, but fleshier than the others. "I'm Abby Pruitt."

"You're right. I've been to the zoo," Frank said. "But I haven't stepped foot in it since we locked it down years ago. I've been in charge of this outpost ever since to make sure nothing gets out the back door. Just like Sarge told me to do."

"You mean you're guarding the back way into the zoo?" Abby asked. This was big news to her.

"Sarge said if I did good he might someday let me take a weekend furlough for good behavior. I could go into town and catch a picture show and mingle with the civilians," Frank said in his cheerful optimistic drawl. "I don't worry too much though. Stan lets me watch all the TV I want. I sure like them TV shows, especially those shows with all the singing and dancing."

"Stan knows you're out here?" Abby asked.

"Stan is my little brother," Frank answered. "He's getting a little long in the tooth as they say."

At the mention of Stan, a voice called out in the building. "Frank! Is there someone in here with you?"

"Over here, Bubba!" Frank called back.

Abby and Frank walked over and met Stan near the front door. "This is my new best bud Bubba," Frank told him.

"Easy, Frank. Little girl your family is looking for you," Stan said to her. "I won't tell them you were trespassing if you won't tell them about Frank here."

"I won't tell them about Frank. They wouldn't believe me any-way." Abby said.

"Why wouldn't they believe you?" Stan asked.

"I know Frank is dead," she said looking at Frank. "My parents don't believe in that sort of thing."

"You know?" Stan asked puzzled. "That doesn't make you want to run off, scared out of your wits?"

"No," Abby said. "I'm not a baby."

"Can she come back and help me around the shop?" Frank asked.

"How 'bout let's make a deal," Stan said to Abby. "If you help me out selling Christmas trees, I will let you visit with Frank."

Abby thought this sounded fun even though she wasn't sure how she could help him. But she knew she needed to talk to Frank and find out what he knew about the zoo. Maybe he could help her and her brothers.

"Okay, Stan, it's a deal," Abby said and shook his hand to seal the deal. "Maybe my brothers can help too. They are stronger than me." she added, volunteering Philip and Sam for manual labor.

"Let's ask your parents first," Stan said.

"Bye, Frank. Hopefully, I'll see you soon," Abby said waving to him as she left with Stan.

"Bye, bye. Come on back now, ya hear!" Frank said in his funny drawl.

Stan and Abby walked past the rows of trim Christmas trees and into the pasture. Mrs. Pruitt, Philip, and Sam watched Mr.

Pruitt launch a nice-looking tree onto the top of the Land Cruiser and tie it down so the wind wouldn't blow it off. Mr. Pruitt was an expert knot maker.

"Found her!" Stan informed her family.

"Where did you get off to?" Mrs. Pruitt asked.

"Um," Abby began, trying to make sure not to mention Frank. "I was admiring Mr. Barr's workshop. He offered me a job."

"If you're willing, I could sure use the help during the holiday season moving these trees. I can pay a little. She mentioned her brothers were hard workers too," Stan said.

Philip and Sam gave Abby a sour look.

"I think that sounds like a good idea," Mr. Pruitt said, as he climbed off the truck. "I was about the same age when I got my first job."

It was settled. Mr. Pruitt would drop them off next Saturday. Abby was excited, but Philip and Sam were not amused. They warmed up to the idea later when she told them about Frank and the back entrance to the zoo. It was the first new clue about the zoo they had found in months.

The Pruitt family said goodbye to Stan Barr, piled into the Land Cruiser, and headed down the dirt road. Mrs. Pruitt insisted they follow the road all the way back to town and avoid the shortcut. The road continued for a few miles and ended near the park downtown, on the other side of Crooked Creek. It turned out that Mr. Pruitt was right about that shortcut after all.

When they got home, Mr. Pruitt unloaded the tree, and after a struggle, attached the red and green stand to the sappy base. Then, the tree was shoved into the living room, while everyone stood back and watched. Finally, Mrs. Pruitt and Abby hung the Christmas ornaments.

The tree looked wonderful set up in the corner of the living room. The colored lights, silver tinsel, and festive ornaments lit the room, filling their thoughts with anticipation and Christmas cheer.

They spent the rest of the evening, cozy and in good spirits, watching television, while never-ending commercials reminded them to get ready for the holidays.

❋❋❋

24

The last week of school before Christmas break went by fast. It was a whirlwind of tests, holiday crafts, and school plays, at least for Abby and Sam who were in elementary school. Philip was in the eight grade. He just tried to stay out of the way of the older kids and social cliques and finish his final exams. He was a little old to enjoy Christmas in the same way as Abby and Sam. Some of the magic was gone.

Philip and Sam were not happy about Abby volunteering them for work at Stan Barr's Christmas tree farm, but by the end of the school week they were ready to get outside, even if it meant doing work.

On a cold and cloudy Saturday, feeling more like December than the previous Saturday, Mr. Pruitt drove to the tree farm and dropped them off. The pasture was crowded with families buying trees. Stan put them immediately to work.

He showed Philip how to cut the trees down with a big bow saw and a few rapid long cuts. Philip got the hang of it after a few trees and soon was as quick as Stan.

Sam's job was to drag the trees through the pasture to the parking area for the families. Then he would help load the trees onto the cars and trucks.

Abby was in charge of collecting the money. Because she liked math, it was the best job for her. Plus, she had fun talking to everyone that came to the tree farm.

Stan turned on flood lights when it got dark. People came in to get trees well into the evening. The air became chilly, and your breath would hang in the air like smoke.

The last family left around 7 o'clock. After closing down, Stan took the kids to the Quonset hut to get warm. Frank was waiting inside. He had set buckets upside down around a black pot belly stove that radiated heat. He was busy frying bologna on a skillet for sandwiches. "I remember this used to be good eatin'," Frank said to the kids when they sat down on the buckets. "Miracle Whip makes it better, I always say," He gobbed it onto each sandwich.

Abby introduced her brothers to Frank as he passed around the fried bologna sandwiches. Frank was happy to make new friends. Philip and Sam eyed the sandwiches.

"Just eat em'. They're good," Frank told them. They ate the sandwiches quickly and were ready for another. Frank made another round and found some cans of soda.

Stan sat down in a nearby chair after he ate and was soon snoring. "He's just takin' a cat nap. He'll wake himself up shortly," Frank said.

"You've got a lot of neat stuff, Frank," Sam said, gazing around the building.

"I have to keep everything working and in tip-top shape. I'm in charge. That's what Sarge said. Make sure that the perimeter is secure," Frank said in his funny drawl. He was serious. "I'm not sure if Sarge is coming back, though. I haven't received any new orders in years."

"Who is Sarge?" Abby asked.

Frank put some more wood in the stove and smoke puffed out when he closed the small door. "I don't know if I can tell you," Frank said, then whispered. "It's National Security."

"It's okay. We won't tell anyone. Who would believe us?" Philip said. "We're the only ones who know you're here."

Frank thought for a moment. "Friends is friends and you can't keep nothing from friends, I always say."

He pulled up a bucket and sat down. "We were stationed here in '44, during the Second World War, to provide support for a secret operation that was going to help the Allies win the war. Right off, something seemed fishy. I didn't pay much mind to it. I just followed orders. Guard the scientists so they could do their work. There were rumors of bizarre things going on, ghoulish experiments, and the dead coming back to life. No way had I believed any of that stuff. Nuh, uh. Then one day I was ordered to take a Half-track, mount an auger to the back of it, of all things, and drill a hole in that darn whopper of a tree. The scientists wanted a core sample."

"We saw that truck!" Abby interrupted. "The tree swallowed it up."

Frank looked surprised. "That was a heck of a time. I drilled all day until the tree just crushed the cab of the truck and I woke up like this. I was dead as a door nail, but I came back. That's when I knew the rumors were true. The scientists were experimenting on the dead animals. And then me too, but I don't want to talk about that. A few months later, in '45, the war ended and Project Ever Fresh was shelved. Sarge ordered me to stay here and make sure nothing got out the back door. Nobody or nothing has ever come through."

"Project Ever Fresh?" Philip said. "Is that what it was called?"

"Yep," Frank said. "The reason we were there was to figure out how to keep MCI's from going bad. You know, to make them stay fresh for a really long time, and maybe, taste better."

"What's a MCI?" Sam asked.

"Meal, Combat, Individual ration. It's food for the battlefield. Most of them taste horrible, but I always ate every last bite of mine," Frank said.

"You mean they went through all that trouble just to preserve food?" Abby was stunned. "I can't believe it."

"Yep. I don't think they succeeded 'cause they never did taste any better." Frank said. He got up and went over to some shelves along the wall. He took down a dusty box and brought it back to his seat. Inside was a stack of papers and notebooks, foxed with age. He dug through the papers until he found what he was looking for. He handed Abby a notebook that had CLASSIFIED stamped on the cover.

"What is it?" Abby asked, opening the book.

"It belonged to the scientist in charge of the project," Frank said. "Dr. Xeno was a real twerp. And these journals he left behind prove it."

Abby read. "November 1st, 1944. After the initial phase, all subjects have been terminated mainly by starvation or dehydration. Those that did not perish within the given period of time were administered gas. I am delighted at the results. All subjects have reanimated with no ill effects. It is a wonder this can occur. I have observed complete disassembly of a dozen animals. Removal of skin, organs, and skeletal disarticulation has been performed. In all cases, the animal, if given time, can regenerate to a functional state."

Abby turned to a different page. "December 9, 1944. Less than stellar results. Each attempt to extract viable animal cells to produce a product capable of stabilizing cell degeneration and eventual death has proved fruitless. Have been reduced to aerosolizing all body fluids from the animals for application to food products. No effect on food preservation, but the soldiers, unaware that they are test subjects, have experienced side effects such as nausea, bloating, intestinal spasms, sensitivity to light, gas, vomiting, explosive stool, mental confusion, and rage. The soldiers are becoming suspicious of our efforts. There is talk among them that we are making them sick with the food. I will have to cut the dosage of preservative for a period. Perhaps we can have them ingest animal protein in its re-animated unaltered state. But I hesitate. Without an end product that can be patented I will have no financial gain and I intend to have fame and wealth."

She turned a few more pages. "December 24, 1944. Depressed. I cannot get the dead animals to feel pain. Suffering, pain, and fear I believe are the only means I have for success. I am desperate for success. I know I can force these beasts to give me their secret. On another note, there appears to be a faint ionized charge to the air around the strange tree on the other side of the zoo. For several nights a faint electrical glow can be seen above it. It reminds me of the aurora borealis. There have been minor earth tremblers in the area.

Perhaps that is the cause. I have instructed some of the soldiers to investigate."

"It goes on and on like this," Abby said. "All those animals were killed and tortured to make food stay fresh." She tossed the journal back in the box. She didn't want to read anymore.

"Why not make zombie super-soldiers?" Sam said. "No one could stop them. That's what I would have done."

"I never thought of that," Frank said. "But it's hard to get motivated when you're dead."

A horn honked outside. Stan woke up with a snort. "We're closed!" he said to no one.

"Sounds like our dad is here," Philip said. "We have to go."

Frank sat by the stove. "See you later," he said, looking disappointed that his friends had to go.

"I'll be right back, Frank," Stan said, getting up. "Your friends will be back in a couple days to help sell trees. There's still plenty to do."

"Don't worry, Frank," Abby said. "We really like hanging out with you. Maybe you can help us with something. We'll tell you about it next week."

"Sure!" he said, perking up.

"See you later," Sam said.

Stan led the kids across the cold, dark pasture toward the glare of the truck lights. Before they jumped into the almost warm cab of the Land Cruiser, Stan said, "Almost forgot." He handed each of them a ten-dollar bill. "Come back on Monday and I'll put you to work. Closed Sunday."

They drove off through the darkness down the dirt road. Mr. Pruitt was in a good mood and was glad they had had a good time. They were tired and didn't talk much on the ride home. Abby's mind worked hard going over everything Frank had said. She didn't know what to do. She just wanted to help her friends at the zoo, but that seemed like an impossible thing. Was it even possible to make things right, to undo what has already been done? She thought about Frank, abandoned along with the zoo. She could feel a glimmer of hope growing within her. Frank was going to help them.

"We're home," Mr. Pruitt said. They got out of the truck and went inside the house. Instead of watching television, Philip and Sam went to their rooms and fell asleep. Abby stayed in the living room with Mrs. Pruitt and watched some shows late into the evening. She was tired, but she had too much to think about before she could sleep.

❊ ❊ ❊

25

The next day the weather turned. The air was heavy all morning, and clouds hung low over the town. The temperature dropped below freezing, and it got colder and colder as the day passed. A winter storm had arrived.

Mr. and Mrs. Pruitt decided this would be the perfect time to go shopping, so they took the Land Cruiser and headed to the Special Member's Shopping Club to stock up on food. Mrs. Pruitt didn't want to get stuck at home in a storm and not be able to feed her family. When they arrived at the store, the giant parking lot was packed full and they had to park far from the store.

"Is it difficult to get into the Special Member's Shopping Club?" Sam asked.

"As long as you're breathing, you can be a member," Mr. Pruitt answered.

Inside, the store was a bustling sea of people. Overloaded shopping carts jostled by as families fought for their place. Mr. Pruitt grabbed a cart and led the charge. A large woman stepped in front of them.

"Are you Special Members?" she demanded sternly.

"Of course, what do we look like, a bunch of 'regular members'?" Mr. Pruitt showed her his Special Member's pass card with his picture on it.

"You check out," She gave them a big sugary sweet smile. "God be with you. Enjoy your shopping experience." Shopping was taken very seriously here. Mrs Pruitt gave the kids a look and rolled her eyes. They giggled as they passed by the stern gaze of the gatekeeper to the bargains.

They followed Mr. Pruitt into the massive food isles. They were bored immediately.

"Can we go look at toys?" Sam asked.

"Sure, we'll meet you there in a bit," Mrs. Pruitt said.

They took off into the crowd. Philip led the way. He took a detour and stopped at the outdoor supply isle filled with camping gear, fishing rods and tackle, and hunting rifles. Philip imagined what he could do if he had all of this gear. He was mesmerized.

"Come on," Sam said. "You have enough worms and sinkers and stupid fishing lures. We need more toys."

"I'll catch up with you," Philip said taking down a fly fishing pole that was on sale.

Abby and Sam left Philip and headed for the toys. It was pure mayhem in the toy department. Kids whined and screeched; parents yelled and caved in to demands. Toys were scattered on the floor or barely hanging on shelves. Abby and Sam jumped into the feeding frenzy. The ten dollars they each earned yesterday at the tree farm wanted to be spent.

Pastor Jasper Newton was standing alone in the isle across from them with a shopping cart, watching them. Abby was the first to see him. She nudged Sam and they both stared back at him. He seemed different. He motioned with his hand for them to come over to him. Cautiously, they went over to meet him.

"I was hoping I would get to talk with you children again," the Pastor said, in a calm, relaxed voice. Something about him was definitely different. He was dressed in normal clothes. His hair was disheveled and he hadn't shaved. His shopping cart was full of packages of bacon.

The Pastor's eyes looked glazed. "What was I going to say?" he said, tuning in to Abby and Sam. "Oh, I remember. I wanted to make amends. I have been unkind to you. That's what I wanted to say."

Abby and Sam were stunned. Was the Pastor apologizing to them for all the crazy things he had said and done? It can't be. "What do you mean?" Sam asked, hoping not to spark a rant from the Pastor.

"I am better now. My medication has allowed me to think more clearly," the Pastor said, glassy-eyed.

"Okay," Abby said cautiously.

"My life has changed. A weight has been lifted," the Pastor told them. "Do you remember what you said to me when we last met?" he asked, looking at Abby.

"Yes," she said. She did remember. "I told you Betty says hello. It didn't mean anything."

"I have thought about what you said on many evenings, and I have remembered things long buried in my mind," the Pastor said. "The medications helped."

"I have something that belongs to the zoo," the Pastor told them. Abby and Sam where shocked at the mention of the zoo.

"It's true. You were at the zoo?" Abby said.

"Yes, I was there, and I know that you've been there, too. I wasn't a very well-adjusted child. I did bad things and I stole something that did not belong to me," he said. "I want to give it to you. Maybe you will know what to do with it."

Abby was interested, but Sam was not convinced that the Pastor had changed. "I don't know," Sam said. "We'll think about it."

"You have to take the thing off my hands. It is a curse to me," the Pastor said. "Come tomorrow, the driveway where you saw me last leads to my daughter's house. I will be there in the morning." They knew the place. Until now, they had not thought about how odd it was to see the Pastor at the Pig Lady's driveway. They just assumed he was nosy. Now it made sense.

Before Abby or Sam could question him further, Philip showed up. Seeing the Pastor, Philip jumped into the isle. "What are you doing here?" Philip demanded.

"It's okay, Philip," Abby said. "He's changed."

"Are you sure?" Philip said.

Pastor Jasper Newton turned his shopping cart around. "I'll be seeing you," he said and headed down the isle.

"What were you thinking?" Philip said. Abby explained what had happened.

Mr. and Mrs. Pruitt interrupted. "Good, you're here," Mr. Pruitt said. "Let's go before the weather strands us. I don't want to spend the night here."

They waited in line at the checkout forever it seemed. Mrs. Pruitt paid the bill while Mr. Pruitt loaded the cart with bags. They forgot to spend the money they earned at the tree farm thanks to the run-in with the Pastor.

They left the store and walked through the parking lot to the Land Cruiser. The afternoon light was fading, and the parking lot was slick with a coat of ice. Tiny ice pellets stung their faces. The sound of tires spinning on the ice and the smell of burning rubber added to the excitement in the air. Everyone in town knew that if they didn't get home soon, it could be catastrophe.

Mr. Pruitt put the truck in four-wheel drive. It was getting colder. The truck rolled away from the turmoil in the parking lot and they headed home. Along the way, cars fishtailed and slide off the road. Mr. Pruitt stopped twice to pull people out of tough spots with the Land Cruiser's winch.

Each time was an ordeal. Mr. Pruitt would pull off the road, unlatch the hood of the truck, open it, pull the steel winch cable out, attach it to the bumper of the car, and then stand on the bumper to operate the winch by a lever next to the motor. The winch dragged each car just as easy as pulling a stick out of the mud.

They finally arrived home just as the heater in the truck was beginning to warm up. Safe inside the house, they watched the ice coat everything in crystal. Trees were soon heavy with ice, limbs bent to the ground from the weight. Loud cracks pierced the dark outside as tree branches finally gave way, crashing to the ground or an unfortunate neighbor's roof. It didn't let up throughout the night.

The electricity went out. They lit candles and the candle light reflected off the ornaments hanging on the Christmas tree, giving the living room a magical glow. Mr. Pruitt started a roaring fire in the fireplace, and that night they slept crowded around the fire to keep warm.

They talked late into the evening while Mr. Pruitt stoked the fire, keeping the flames high. Occasionally, they would rush to the windows when a particularly loud branch would break away and crash down. What if a tree fell through their roof? What if the Land Cruiser got smashed by an out-of-control car on the icy street? What if a tree branch busted through a window? None of these things happened to the Pruitt family this evening, though they happened to many other families. They were safe and sound, huddled around the fireplace, during the worst ice storm to hit Forest Heights in a hundred years.

* * *

26

The electricity was still out the next morning. The ice storm had ended, and the sun was shining bright in a clear blue sky. The sun reflecting on the ice-covered world was blinding. Branches lay everywhere, trees entombed in ice bowed to the ground while the stoutest trees were split and mangled and lay in the streets, on cars, and houses. Power lines were draped in ice and hung in arcs to the ground. It was quiet and nothing moved. The town was shut down, and they were shut in. Philip, Sam, and Abby had to get out and explore.

Mrs. Pruitt set up a camp stove just outside the kitchen door and soon had a breakfast of eggs and sausage prepared, and Mr. Pruitt was able to have his morning coffee. He set to work clearing a path to the truck. It was a mess. The truck was frozen solid in a shell of ice, and the door handles would not budge. He decided to get wood for the fireplace instead and let the sun melt the ice.

Stomachs full, Philip, Sam, and Abby scrambled to get into their warmest clothes. First, thermal underwear, two pairs of socks, three shirts each, a coat, and boots. Abby added green and red earmuffs, Philip pulled a bright hunter orange knit cap over ears, and Sam found a hunting cap with furry earflaps.

"Bye, Mom!" they yelled as they ran out the front door not bothering to close it behind them. Mr. Pruitt was busy splitting logs with an ax in the front yard. "Don't go too far!" Mr. Pruitt yelled as he sank the ax into a dried out log. "And watch for power lines!"

Philip and Abby slid down the driveway, hunching over with their arms spread wide, trying to stay upright. Sam crunched through the icy yard to the side of the house to get his sled. It was frozen tight to the ground. He stomped as hard as he could to free it, but it wouldn't budge. He gave up and slid out of the yard and into the street after Philip and Abby.

There was an unspoken plan between the three of them. They were going to meet Pastor Jasper Newton today. He had something for them and they wanted to find out what it was. But they still didn't trust him.

They made it to the street corner and were about to head down the next street when Abby's legs suddenly swung out from under her and she landed on her back. She slid back down the street clutching at the slick ice and trying to stop. Faster and faster she went. She shot past their house, bounced over the curb, and barreled off into the ice choked woods on the far side of the street.

Philip and Sam looked at each other, dumbfounded. "Why does Abby have to be so dramatic all the time?" Sam asked. Philip shrugged. They went after her, on foot at first, then sliding by the seat of their pants down to where Abby disappeared. She had punched a hole through a tangle of icy rose bushes with her body on her way down a gulley at the side of a neighbor's yard. She was nowhere to be seen.

"Well, let's go find the drama queen," Philip said. Sam lowered himself over the curb and slipped through the bramble and out of sight with a fading whoop. Philip grabbed a branch for support, but he lost his footing and went down the gulley on his stomach.

Abby sat up, her leg dangled over a ledge of rock. She pulled herself back and stood up. Icy green ferns, moss, and lichen grew around the ledge. She looked over it at the stream below flowing from a dark cave. She was amazed that she had never seen this wonderful place.

Abby had only a moment to take notice of her surroundings before her brothers came barreling down the hill and crunched to a landing next to her. Ice flew everywhere.

It was twenty feet or so to the stream below. The water flowed from deep under the ledge and into a nice deep pool covered in thick ice. The stream rushed from pool to pool down the narrow gulley, between boulders and bent over trees. Water flowed beneath the ice, bubbling and clear.

To crawl back up the hill to the street would take forever they decided. The newly found stream looked too inviting. Holding onto roots and trees and sliding between boulders they made their way down to the edge of the big pool.

Sam walked out onto the frozen pool without a care. The ice was thick and didn't break. He jumped on it to prove his point. Abby and Philip skated out watching the water bubble beneath the rock solid ice. When they stomped on the ice, it sounded hard and hollow and it shook the water below.

Sam skated under the ledge to the edge of the ice daring it to break under his feet, but it held his weight. They laughed and played for awhile. The stream seemed to want them to follow it down the gulley so they did.

They skated from pool to pool along the frozen stream. The gulley became a little valley with ice covered ruins of an old mill and long gone buildings. They marveled at the ruins where they camped one summer night over three months ago. They skated on and on, laughing and playing, forgetting about the world, until they saw a column of black, greasy smoke rising off in the woods.

They left the stream, skirted around a hill, and found themselves at a fence with a cattle guard lying across a trail. A pristine field, coated in ice, with a couple of walnut trees and a rickety old cabin at one end, spread out before them. A black column of smoke belched from the cabin's chimney.

"I've been here!" Abby said. "Where are the pigs?"

Smoke billowed from the chimney like a furnace of hell. There was no sign of pigs or the crazed Pig Lady, so they marched across the field. A car, coated in ice, was parked next to the cabin. They walked up the wood plank steps and onto the worn thin porch.

They could hear someone stomping back and forth through the cabin. They were scared. They thought about running back to the solitude of the stream. Before they could decide what to do, the door opened and Pastor Jasper Newton stood there wild-eyed and manic.

"How about that!" he said. "The early bird gets the worm!" he paused and scrunched his face in strange thought. "Or is it the other way round? I forget. Anyway, you're just in time, or too late, it's hard to say!" He seemed to have gone mad. "Come in, come in, and let's find out."

They followed him into the cabin, and he shut the door. The air inside was like an oven. The Pastor was in a dark mood. He snatched up a wooden chair and broke the legs from it, thrusting the pieces into the roaring inferno in the fireplace, a stone monument at one end of the room. The stones glowed from the immense heat. The Pastor did not seem to notice as he continued to cast everything within reach into the flames: spoons, forks, plates, books, a phone, pictures hanging on the wall, clothes. He shoved everything in. The fire consumed it all and licked the stone mantle. Flames leapt from the fireplace into the room and black smoke curled from the mouth and then quickly pulled back into the chimney.

"You kept your word," the Pastor said. "I forgot about that zoo, blocked it out, but it flooded back. I felt relief. Then, I remembered. I took something that didn't belong to me." He struggled with his thoughts.

He stared at the fire, lost in the flames. "The souls at the zoo are cursed. I hated them. It was the Devil at work. My faith was being tested. So, I found my way to the secret heart of the zoo, to a spring within the giant tree, and asked God to save my soul."

"A voice in my mind told me to reach into the water of the spring and pull forth the thorn of existence. I plunged my hand beneath the water, blind to all but faith, and brought forth a stone. The ground shook and the spring trembled. I fled with the stone, thinking I had cast the Devil aside, tricked him as he tricked mankind. But it was I that was tricked. I alone am the Devil to myself." The Pastor threw the last of the furniture into the fire. The room was now bare.

The Pastor took a prescription bottle from his pocket; considered opening it, then threw it in the fire. He strode over to a bedroom door and opened it wide. He down next to a sunken bed covered with a patchwork quilt. His giant daughter lay dead on the bed. He retrieved a cigar box from under the bed, tucked it under his arm, and kissed his daughter on her forehead. "My precious daughter, the only thing that mattered to me, now gone forever. She passed last night. Heartbroken, ever since she ate her last and favorite pig."

A window pane cracked loudly from the heat and shattered on the floor. The flames consumed the fresh air instantly and engulfed the inside of the cabin.

Abby jumped forward, grabbed the cigar box, and bounded to the front door. She flung it open and ran out leaving Philip and Sam stunned for a moment. Then they bolted after her while the tortured Pastor still knelt at his daughter's bedside.

They slammed down the front steps and slid and stumbled far out into the icy field. They lay on the ground taking in the cold, clean air.

The cabin breathed flames. Black smoke rolled out through the cracks in the settled beams of the structure. Windows melted, the porch burned, then the roof collapsed. Pastor Jasper Newton was dead. He went with his daughter toward whatever waited beyond the flames and smoke.

Abby opened the battered cigar box. Inside was a stone figure of a dog sitting on its haunch with its tail curled to one side. The stone was tan in color and the features were smooth. It was the match to the figurine of a person that they had seen in the spring. It must mean something.

"What do we do with it?" Philip wondered.

"We take it back to its home," Abby said. "To the spring in the zoo. Maybe it will change the animals back from being zombies. I think the other figurine changed the people back to normal, why not a figurine for the animals."

Urgent sirens wailed from the fire station across town. The sirens grew louder coming toward the smoke billowing from the burning cabin. They didn't know what to do. Afraid of what their parents would think, they panicked and ran away.

They ran across the field and into the woods. They found the stream again and clambered and slid all the way down it to a bridge. They climbed up to the street above and found themselves in the historic district near the town square.

They walked through the quaint old neighborhood, past grand old Victorian houses from another era. It was still morning and not many households stirred. Black smoke hung in the sky behind them.

A particular house, with a low brick wall and an iron gate, was almost hidden from the street. A mailbox caught Abby's eye. It read, "Meanwell". She knew this name and appreciated its significance.

Philip and Sam walked on while Abby tried the gate. It swung inward. A path led to a large ancient brick mansion with tall windows.

Abby walked down the path and pressed a button next to the door that activated a buzzer inside the house. Philip and Sam slid back on the sidewalk and bustled down the path to see what Abby was up to.

After a moment, a lock clunked and the door squeaked open. An old woman bundled in an ancient fur coat gazed at them. She was bent and short. Her face peaked shrewdly from the dark brown fur.

"Yes?" she asked. "Is there something the matter?"

"Are you related to Thomas Meanwell?" Abby asked. "I know this may sound strange, but I just thought I would ask."

The old woman, older than old, octogenarian or maybe centurion, looked shocked and stepped back. "Who sent you? Did he send you?" she asked in a surprisingly authoritative voice.

"No one sent us. If you don't know Thomas, then we will leave," Abby said. Before they could turn and continue on their way, the old woman said, "Thomas was a fool. Come in, out of the cold, though it isn't much warmer in here. The power is out."

The house was full of beautiful, fine things. Crystal chandeliers, dark, plush furniture, and all draped in velvet and frilly lace, gaudy. Expensive in the last century, but now antique.

The old lady led them to a closed room at the back of the house. The room had many tall windows that came almost to the floor and let in a wonderful view of the crystallized yard. Tree limbs coated in ice leaned against the glass.

A steady fire glowed in the old fireplace. The room was quite austere, except for a stuffed chair and a little table, all cozy near the warmth of the hearth, and a tremendous pile of firewood crowding the room. The smell of smoke and saw dust, and mildew on old furniture and drafty floor boards, was pleasant.

"Throw another log on would you young man," the lady said to Philip. Philip did so.

"So, tell us about Thomas Meanwell," Abby said, she was beginning to feel irritated and a little strange. Sam stepped in, noticing his sister was getting cranky, "What's your name, lady?"

"I am Isabella Meanwell, a widow too old to be thinking about such things so long ago. Why is your little friend looking so pale?" she asked looking at Abby.

"Her name is Abby, and she's our sister," Philip said. Abby sat hard on the floor and put her head in her hands and started to cry.

"Good gracious!" said Mrs. Meanwell. Philip and Sam bent over her and did the best they could to console her. They felt it too—the raw nerves, the shock of watching Pastor Jasper Newton burn himself up. Abby felt it the most, she always did.

"I'm okay," Abby said, wiping her eyes on her coat sleeve. She got up and stood in front of Isabella Meanwell. "We need help," Abby said.

"What do you mean?" Mrs. Meanwell asked with a shrewd look on her wealthy, wrinkled, puckered old face.

"We've been to the zoo. They're all still there," Abby said. "You're husband, Thomas, was there, the animals, all the people who died, they are still walking around, forgotten."

"If you met Thomas, then you must know that I cared for him?" Isabella said.

"He told us you never forgave him. You knew he was still there, why did you leave him?" Abby asked.

"He was dead, young lady," Mrs. Meanwell said. "The natural order was broken, no matter how much he meant to me. I should never have married him, anyway. He was a monster."

"He wasn't a monster!" Abby said. "You turned him into a monster. He tried to end it all, and he did turn into a monster. He almost killed us! Me and my brothers! But now he is gone. He's dead!"

"I'm sorry you found that dread zoo," Mrs. Meanwell said, her voice rising. "I can't help you. Thomas was beneath me, you children are beneath me. Leave my home and never come back!"

They left Isabella Meanwell, wrapped in her fur coat, boiling mad in her cold house. Abby stormed out the front door. She was mad and it wasn't like her to be like this.

She stomped down the path to the front gate, threw it open, and stomped down the sidewalk, leaving her brothers behind. She was so mad. Why is that old lady so mean? Does being rich make you not care about anyone other than yourself? What's wrong with everyone? She fumed in her head.

"Leave me alone!" she yelled back at Philip and Sam when they asked if she was okay. They left her alone and watched her walk down the frozen sidewalk, not sure what to do.

Isabella Meanwell, older than old, dialed a number on the telephone. "Tell me why three children just came by my home and asked me about my long dead husband?" There was a pause. "Yes, just now! You're right you should be sorry! I will not have my finances be questioned because of some silly children!" There was another pause, and apologies. "Take care of it. We will not speak of this again." She hung up. Nothing would come between her and her money. She couldn't believe she was even thinking about this now. It was a lifetime ago. She sunk down into her chair.

***

27

Abby walked down the sidewalk alone. Branches creaked and settled under their burden of ice. The air was still. She turned to see if her brothers followed. She thought she saw a glimpse of Philip's orange hat, but she wasn't sure. No matter. She didn't care anyway, she told herself.

She kept walking until she reached the town square. No one had bothered to come out of their homes to go to work today. She was the only person on the square. She sat down on an icy bench in front of the court house. She ignored the cold seeping through her pants.

She needed to calm down. She put her face in her hands and felt the softness of her gloves and her warm breath. Several minutes passed. She felt less frustrated. She pictured the figurine of the little dog tucked in her coat pocket. She didn't want to look at it ever again.

Through the darkness of her gloves, she heard a voice. "Why so glum little girl?" Abby lifted her head. A man stood in front of her. He was short, with a stern gaze, hair cropped flat on top, waxy skin, black shiny boots, and his shirt was buttoned all the way to the top. He sat down next to her, invading her personal space.

"What could make a lovely little girl like you so blue?" She was uncomfortable with his closeness. She got up to leave, but the man grabbed her by the wrist.

"How about a story?" he asked. "Once, there were some kids that bothered an old lady. The lady called her brother and yelled at him, which made him very mad. He's the one that tells people what to do, not the other way around. So this man, lets call him Sarge, has to do some damage control. He has to make some children disappear. That's his specialty, making things disappear."

"Let go!" Abby yelled.

Suddenly, Philip ran full on from across the street and knocked the man square on the forehead with a broken limb. The force of the blow knocked the man's head right off his neck and it landed in the bushes under the eave of the courthouse. Philip was astonished.

The headless man still held Abby. Then, Sam charged, knocking the man over the bench and flat on his back.

"I hate kids," the head said. Philip picked up an icicle in one hand and the head in the other. He held the icicle ominously above the man's head.

"Doesn't anybody ever stay dead in this town anymore?" Philip said.

The headless body stood up behind the bench and lurched toward Philip. Philip tossed the head to Sam. The body turned and went toward him. Sam tossed the head back to Philip.

"Stop or I'll jam this icicle into your brain!" Philip yelled.

"Okay, okay, you little monster," the head said. The body sat down reluctantly on the bench.

"He said his name is Sarge and Mrs. Meanwell is his sister. She told him to get rid of us." Abby said. "Why would you even care what she wanted? You're dead."

"Pride and duty. I do what I'm told and I enjoy it no matter what. I am here to serve," the head said. The body saluted an empty space.

Philip looked at Abby. "I have an idea. Let's take Sarge back to Mrs. Meanwell's house and see what she thinks."

They marched the headless body of Sarge from the town square. Abby and Sam walked on either side of Philip. Philip carried the head under his arm with the icicle held dangerously close so Sarge could understand the threat. They marched all the way back to the house of Isabella Meanwell.

Abby knocked on the door. Mrs. Meanwell opened it and looked shocked at the sight of the headless man in her doorway. The headless body pushed past the old woman and the children followed.

"Tell us what's going on!" Philip said to Isabella Meanwell.

"Why would you do this to us?" Abby said. "We just wanted to help, and you send your brother to hurt us."

"You want to take my freedom away." the old woman said. She retreated into herself and was quiet.

"Tell us why your head came off," Sam said.

Philip propped the head on a table. "You aren't the first to knock this old melon in the dirt, but I always get back up and keep marching strong." He sounded confident for a head on a table.

"That last day at the zoo, I thought I was done with the place. We secured the perimeter. Everything was locked up tight. No person and no animal escaped. The day started perfect, clean pressed trousers, a smooth shave, fifty push-ups, then coordinating personnel movements, giving orders, and some harmless collateral damage." His body saluted out of reflex. "Then, wouldn't you know, I died. Some puke private called Barr had the choke set too high on the carburetor of his Half-track. I ordered him to stop and let me see the motor. Then, Wham! The hood slammed down and popped my head clean off." He had a gleam in his eye.

"I woke up with a stiff neck, stitches, and went back to war. I fought in every war for the last forty years. You can kill a lot of people when no one can kill you." Sarge looked proud. "But it wasn't the same anymore, so I retired."

"We can help you," Abby said. "We're going to try to put things back the way they should be."

Sarge laughed. "Things are as they should be."

"If you don't leave us alone we're going to hide your head where you will never find it," Abby said.

"I can keep this up for eternity," Sarge said.

"In that case, we can't let you get in our way," Philip said. He picked the head up off the table.

The headless body lunged at Philip to retrieve its head, stumbling and bumping into furniture.

Mrs. Meanwell cringed away from the children. They were beneath her and an utter annoyance. She would let her brother do what he wished to protect her and her property.

"You can't win," the head said. "Just give me back to my body, and we can talk about this reasonably."

Philip didn't want to take the head with them and be forced to listen to it condescend to them. He tossed the head across the room. It bounced off a chair and rolled under a couch. The head cried out, muffled by the cushions and years of dust balls, "This is not proper military protocol."

Philip, Sam, and Abby bolted for the front door and ran down the icy sidewalk to the street. They had had enough. They ran as fast as they could up the icy street and around the next corner. Street after street they ran and slid, until finally, they arrived home.

The power was still out and Mr. and Mrs. Pruitt sat by the fireplace in the living room tending the fire.

"How does the neighborhood look?" Mr. Pruitt asked.

"Uh, okay," they mumbled.

"Did you have fun?" Mrs. Pruitt asked.

"Sure," Philip said, noncommittal.

"Are you hungry?" Mrs. Pruitt asked.

No response.

"I'll make some sandwiches just in case," she said.

Just as the sun set and before another night of frigid cold, the electricity jolted back and the house came back to life. Lights blinked on and the television buzzed awake. The family cheered and everything felt normal for a while.

***

28

The days ahead were cool and windy and the ice melted leaving the ground wet and the streets muddy. Mr. Pruitt kept them busy clearing the yard of branches. The town was free of the ice storm.

On the trips to the grocery store or the mall, Philip, Sam, and Abby would look over their shoulders imagining someone was watching them. They never saw Sarge but they knew he was around.

The passing of Pastor Jasper Newton and his daughter was mentioned on the evening news. The blackened ruins of the cabin flashed on the television screen. The stone chimney stood over the ruins like a grave marker. His faithful flock from the Church of the Holy Harvest mourned and insisted there had never been a truer person, a kinder father. The fire was determined to have been an accident.

Abby spent the evenings in the corner of the living room hidden under the Christmas tree with the lights twinkling brightly. She sat quietly, cross-legged, reading to take her mind off things; her gaze would drift from her book into the branches of the glowing tree. Her dreams floated into the sweet smelling cedar with its gold, red, blue, and green lights. And, of course, her gaze also drifted to the snowy cover at the base with presents neatly wrapped.

Abby felt safe under the tree with her books. No one seemed to notice her while she thought about many things. And that was just fine, since she had a lot to think about.

Philip and Sam had a lot to think about too, but they did it differently. They hung around Mr. Pruitt in the basement while he tinkered with furniture.

For inspiration Abby brought Steve Gerbil with her under the tree. Steve watched Abby from a clear plastic pet ball. Sam had moved him to the ball from the Lego castle after Steve had nearly broken through the dungeon walls. Abby would occasionally look at Steve and wonder if she could really help the undead creature. She thought of the stone figurine of the sitting dog, which she kept in her pant's pocket. That little dog had to be the answer.

She liked to look at Steve Gerbil in his plastic globe. His expression never changed. He always stared, glassy-eyed and deadly, but under the tree the Christmas lights seemed to soften him, and she could see the sweet animal soul in his eyes ready to be restored.

She put the book she was reading aside and stood up to stretch her legs and look out the window. It was evening, but it was bright outside with snow. Snow fell heavily covering the yard and softly blanketing all the trees and bushes. The longer she stared out the window, the more excited she became. It was going to be a white Christmas this year.

As a matter of fact, it was Christmas Eve, the night before Christmas. The snow filled her with happiness and the cheerful lights reflecting off the window glass made her glow. She glanced down at the zombie gerbil watching her, and her spirits sank back to reality. She plopped down on the carpet in her secluded corner under the fragrant cedar tree.

Then something peculiar happened. The Christmas tree shook and a shower of needles pelted her head. The water in the tree stand sloshed and spilled. She watched as roots appeared from the bottom of the tree, knocking off the stand, and spreading across the living room floor. The roots searched for a hold on the carpet and then the tree moved forward. Ornaments fell to the floor. Abby backed further into the corner. The tree moved across the room on roots that writhed and twisted, dragging an extension cord, which was still plugged into the wall.

Abby knew immediately that the force that brought the animals back to life had brought the tree back to life. She knew the tree was searching for anything alive.

The tree searched with its tentacle roots. The extension cord trailing behind it knocked a lamp over with a loud crash.

"What are you doing in there Abby?" Mrs. Pruitt asked from her bedroom. "Are you getting into the Christmas presents?"

The tree followed her voice, heading for the hallway. The tree was stopped by the extension cord still plugged into its socket. Mrs. Pruitt screamed when she saw the roots coiling and writhing under the Christmas tree. Mr. Pruitt heard the scream and ran up the basement stairs. Philip and Sam were close behind him.

The extension cord came loose and the tree lunged forward. Mr. Pruitt took Mrs. Pruitt by the hand and pulled her into the bedroom, slamming the door shut on the top of the tree. The hallway in front of the bedroom was now a tangle of roots and Christmas lights.

"Mom, Dad!" Abby yelled. "Are you all right?"

"Abby, what's going on?" Mr. Pruitt yelled

"We're trapped!" Mrs. Pruitt yelled. "Be careful!"

"We're okay," Philip yelled back.

"Why is the Christmas tree in the hall?" Sam asked.

"Kids, call for help!" Mrs. Pruitt yelled.

Philip raced to the phone hanging on the wall in the kitchen. There was no dial-tone.

"Phone's dead!" Philip yelled back.

"You guys have to go get help!" Mr. Pruitt said.

"Wear warm clothes and watch after your sister!" Mrs. Pruitt said from behind the door.

They forgot all about Christmas Eve. Philip, Sam, and Abby put on boots, gloves, hats, and heavy coats. Philip and Sam didn't know what to do, but Abby knew. She grabbed a shoulder bag and put some supplies in it along with the clear plastic globe that held Steve Gerbil. The stone figurine of the dog was still safe in her pocket.

"We're going to the zoo tonight and ending this," Abby told her brothers. "It's the only way to save mom and dad."

"We can't go now," Philip said. "It's late and it's snowing. We can chop that tree with an ax."

"Everyone in town has one of those trees," Sam said. "Do you think they all came back to life?"

They heard screams outside from the neighborhood and the distant sound of sirens blaring.

"I would say yes," Philip said.

"No one can stop this but us," Abby said. "The trees must have come back to life because they were so close to the zoo. That's got to be it."

Abby ran back to the hallway. "Mom, dad, we'll be back as soon as we can. Help is on its way," Abby said. "Don't worry about us. We'll be with friends."

They went out through the kitchen door into the night. The snow fell heavily, silently, tickling their noses and fluttering across their faces. They felt a rush of exhilaration. The air was cold, but the snow seemed to give them warmth.

Sounds of alarm came from the houses in the neighborhood—shouts, screams, and things crashing, breaking. Forest Heights was getting a Christmas surprise it didn't expect.

As they walked to the street, the snow made a soft sound under their boots—scrunch, scrunch, scrunch. It was up to the tops of their boots and would soon be deeper.

"We can't get far in this snow, Abby," Philip said.

"Maybe I should stay here," Sam volunteered.

"No, you're coming with us," Philip said.

"Shhh," Abby shushed. "Do you hear that?"

There was a noise becoming louder in the distance, a different noise from the panic in the neighborhood. The sound whirred and groaned in the night. Lights flashed between trees several streets away. The lights turned up their street, blinding them, and a massive shape roared up the street headed right for them.

It looked like a ship sailing out of the night, but it had four wheels. The motor thundered and roared. It rolled to a stop in front of their house, idling, and exhaust stinking.

Private Frank Ulysses Barr stood up on the deck and waved to them.

"Hey, ya'll!" He said as friendly as can be. "Waitin' long?" He laughed hard and slapped his knee. "That's a goodun'. I just knew you needed help. Those trees are actin' funny. I think we might have sold a few horse apples, if you know what I mean."

"Frank!" They yelled, relieved and happy to see his round, cheerful face.

"Climb on up," Frank walked to the back of the duck and helped them up a short ladder onto the deck.

"Where's Stan?" Abby asked.

"Oh, his ticker went on the fritz during the ice storm and the Lord plum near took him to heaven," Frank said. "He's restin' at the hospital. I can't blame him. I'd lay down myself, if I could. I'm tired. But I can't rest. I think the Lord wants me to stay here on earth to help you children."

"Maybe," Abby said.

"You better believe it," Frank said. "If I wasn't here now, then how do you think you were gonna' get to were you were goin'?"

"You know we're going to the zoo?" Philip said.

"Sure," Frank said. "I ain't stupid."

Frank sat in the driver's seat, put the vehicle in gear, revved the engine, and launched the duck forward, turning around in a neighbor's yard, and heading back the way he came. Philip, Sam, and Abby held on anyway they could. Things were serious now. It was time for action. They were going back to the zoo.

❊❊❊

29

Frank steered the duck through the blizzard of snow on the streets. Exhaust filled their noses from the back draft on the open deck. The bright headlights blazed.

The rumbled through town, over the bridge at Crooked Creek, past the old train depot, and turned down a long, dirt road that led to the Christmas tree farm.

It was beautiful in the snow, eerie and lonely, pristine. Abby thought she saw a light behind them.

Frank drove through the pasture to the Quonset hut and through a wide doorway at the far end. Once in the building, he shut off the motor, climbed down the ladder on the side, and helped them down. He led the way to the pot belly stove and quickly stoked the fire.

"Ya'll get warm," Frank said. "It's gonna be a long night, I think."

A loud sputtering noise outside the building distracted them. Sarge puttered into the building through the open doorway riding a little blue scooter. He scooted up to them, killing the engine, and put the kickstand down. He wore his military uniform.

Frank stood at attention, clicking his heels together and saluting severely out of habit.

"Private Barr, I see you are aiding the enemy," Sarge drilled. "Explain your actions."

"We are attempting to protect the people of Forest Heights, sir," Frank responded. "I am fully within orders, sir."

Sarge's head was badly sewn back to his neck.

"At ease Private Barr," Sarge said. "You are relieved of duty."

"No, sir," Frank said. "My duty is to my friends."

Sarge marched past Frank toward the kids who crowded behind the stove.

Frank could not stand by and take orders from his demented, authoritarian Sergeant. His duty to friends and family came first.

"Sarge, If you touch those kids, I'm gonna have to pull rank," Frank said. Sarge ignored him, so, Frank did what he had to do. He picked up a shovel and for third time in Sarge's life, his head was knocked clean off his neck.

His head bounced and rolled across the concrete floor. The body tripped and fell forward landing on the floor. Philip and Sam held him down.

Frank scooped up Sarge's head with the shovel.

"This will give you time to think about what you've done, sir" Frank said. He dropped the head in an ammo box and clamped the lid shut. Then he hog-tied Sarge's body.

"Show us the back door to the zoo, Frank," Abby said. "Before something else happens."

Frank led them away from the Quonset hut. The ghostly glow from the snow gave them enough light to see the way. They marched through the deep soft snow into the forest and stopped at a tall, chain link gate with razor wire coiled on top. The gate blocked a gap where a section of the massive rock wall surrounding the zoo had been demolished.

Frank went to one side and unlocked a padlock. He pushed the gate aside so they could pass through. Philip, Sam, and Abby squeezed through the gate, and Frank closed it between them. He smiled at them through the chain link.

"I can't go with you," he said. "I have to make sure nothing gets out of the zoo. I'll wait here for a while, but I need to go back and make sure Sarge doesn't get loose. He's dangerous. Come back and see me when you finish. You guys are the best friends I ever had." They wanted to beg him to come with them but they knew he was right.

"We'll see you, soon," Abby said.

Frank stopped her. "Take this." He handed her a short, odd looking pistol.

"It's a flare gun," he said. "If something goes wrong, shoot it in the air and I'll be there in no time flat."

Abby took the gun and put it in her shoulder bag.

The three of them hiked into the forest beyond the gate leaving Frank clutching the fence as he watched them leave.

Snow fell and coated their hats and gloves. They were too excited to feel the cold. The silence was nearly perfect, except for the constant flitter of snow flakes falling to the forest floor through the dark branches overhead.

They trudged through the snow, not sure where they were or where they were going. They just let themselves be drawn toward the center of the zoo.

They came upon a clearing in the forest. The silhouette of a log cabin with a glowing window sat in the clearing. Smoke lingered above the chimney. It looked inviting.

"Who could be living out here?" Sam wondered. "Don't they know about the zombies?"

They crept up to the cabin window and looked in. There was a kitchen table, a fire place, a bed at the far wall, a few chairs, a chest against a wall, and little else in the small, one-room home.

"Christmas gifts! Christmas gifts!" happy, young voices cheered behind them.

"Looks that way," a man with a deep voice said.

They jumped, startled at the voices.

A tall, black man stood before them, his two children, a boy and girl, and his wife. He carried a freshly cut cedar tree over his shoulder and his wife carried an ax.

His wife opened the door and his children ran inside. "Quit your gawking and come in. Visitors on Christmas Eve are rare indeed," the kind man said. He waited a moment until they entered the cozy home.

The man set the tree end first into a large stoneware jug near the hearth.

"Why hasn't your tree come back to life," Abby spoke up.

"Trees don't come back to life," the man said. "Only people and the animals get to come back, to make amends for what they have done in this life."

"But," she started, confused and trying to think of a reason why the tree farm trees came to life and this one didn't. She couldn't make the connection.

"Oh, you're dead too," Sam said.

"We are," the man said. "But don't worry, we are good people. I hope you brought gifts on this blessed evening."

"Where are my manners?" the lady said. "I'm Fannie Cobb, my fine husband, Joseph Cobb, and our two delightful children, Rose and Jack."

Rose held out her hand to Abby, "I'm Rose," she said. "I'm five years old, Jack is seven. You're pretty."

"I'm Abby, and that's Philip and Sam, my silly brothers," She told her.

"I've been five years old ever since I can remember," Rose said. "Did you bring us gifts?"

"Uh," Abby said.

"Rose, that's not polite," Fannie said.

"She isn't used to visitors and neither are we," Fannie said. "It's been years and years. But, Rose is right. All guests on Christmas Eve have to give a gift."

Rose joined her brother Jack at the Christmas tree and decorated it with bright colored stones, carved trinkets, bright red berries from dogwood trees, and special, pretty things collected over the years. They hung their stockings on the fireplace mantle and lit candles in red and green glass holders.

Fannie and Joseph sat down at the kitchen table in the middle of the room. Philip, Sam, and Abby joined them.

"So, why are three, white children out in the middle of a snow storm, away from their family, and not a bit concerned that they are talking to a family long dead," Joseph asked.

"We are on our way to the Great Tree," Abby said. "We are going to put everything back the way it was."

"What do you propose to do at the Big Tree?" Fannie asked.

"We are going to put *this* in the spring," Abby took the small dog figurine from her pocket and put it on the table.

Joseph picked it up and looked at it closely. "It looks old, but I don't see what it can do." He handed the figurine back to Abby.

Rose and Jack burst out, "Is that a gift for us?"

"No," Fannie said. "But I'm sure they have something for you."

Abby had an idea. She opened her shoulder bag and took out the clear plastic ball with Steve Gerbil inside. She held him up for Rose and Jack to see. The kids were awestruck. Joseph and Fannie looked curious.

"What is that?" Rose said.

"This is Steve. Don't let him out, ever. He's only cute to look at," Abby said.

Rose took the ball and put it on the floor. Steve Gerbil rolled it across the floor. Rose and Jack laughed and clapped ecstatically and followed the gerbil through the room.

"Strange gift," Fannie said.

"We must give you a gift as well," Joseph said. "But first I think you should know our story."

"A long time ago, there was no zoo here," Joseph began. "This was a plantation. Black folk like us worked the land by force. Many people died and many people suffered, like us, for a long time. Then, we were free. The plantation burned and people moved away. And a zoo was built on this land."

"Why did you stay?" Philip asked.

"To keep our home and family together," Joseph said. "To be a slave wounds you deeply. We died wrongly, by the greed of others, but for over a hundred years we have lived unnoticed and happy. That is how you have come to find us here."

Philip, Sam, and Abby told them what they knew of the zoo.

"What you say is dire," Joseph said. "And I wish to help you. I remember what it meant to be alive and in need. It is a terrible thing when no one will help you." They were moved by Joseph's words and his pledge to help.

They watched as Rose and Jack were now being chased around the room by the plastic globe with the angry gerbil inside. The simple Christmas Eve in the cabin made them feel at home and comfortable.

"I think there is someone you should meet," Joseph said. "He has been here much longer than us. We do not speak of him because he is very difficult to be around. I believe he can help you."

"Not him," Fannie said. "He can't help anyone."

"Who can't help us," Philip asked.

"We don't speak his name," Joseph said. "We call him White Devil. He cares for no one. His people left him many centuries ago."

"White Devil," Sam said. "I like the sound of that."

❊❊❊

30

They said goodbye to Fannie, Rose, and Jack. Abby found two red and white stripe candy canes in her shoulder bag and gave them to Rose and Jack.

Joseph led them from the cabin into the winter night. The snow had stopped, and it felt colder. They pulled their coats tight and their hats close over their ears.

They walked up a tall, conical hill that rose just high enough to see the surrounding land. On a clear day, one would be able to see everything that went on at the zoo. They came to a peak, narrow on all sides and rocky, with barely a foothold. A shelf of rock jutted from the peak. An impossible feat of nature had left this jagged block of stone a millions years ago.

Joseph stopped at a snow drift at the outcrop of rock.

"White Devil, come out, its Christmas Eve!" Joseph called to the drift of snow. No answer. He reached into the snow and began digging by hand. Finally, the snow drift shifted and collapsed revealing a hollow cut into the face of the rock. A still figure sat in the grotto.

The moon peaked out from behind the last snow cloud in the sky and lit up the hill top. The man's skin was thin to his bones and he wore a crested metal helmet. He had a pointed beard, and ancient tattered clothes clung to his body. A sword, as well as a long, formidable halberd, lay at his side. The man spoke to them in Spanish.

"English, White Devil!" Joseph said. "Speak English."

"Why do you bother me, I was thinking of days long gone," the man said.

"Be kind, White Devil, or I will stick you under a rock where you will never see the light of day," Joseph said. "I brought you guests. You might help them."

The man scanned the kids with cloudy eyes.

"Come closer, step up," he said. "I cannot move a muscle or even a finger. I am fused together and cannot bend a joint. My bones have betrayed me."

They stepped up and stood in front of him so he could get a better look.

"Live children!" he said in Spanish, then in English. "Oh, I remember what it was like to be spry and young. It has to be nearly 500 years now."

"That's a long time ago," Sam said, not sure what else to say to the strange immobile man.

"That is an understatement boy," he said.

"Why can't you move?" Abby asked.

"If you have nothing to do but sit for five centuries, your joints turn to stone and you can't move," he said.

"Why do they call you, White Devil?" Philip asked, eyeing the sword and halberd.

The man's eyes narrowed dangerously. "Boy, I am a devil like none you have met. I am Hernando De Soto, the conquistador, come to find gold and land for my country. I killed hundreds of men and women and children, all heathen and godless, all by this sword at my side, in the name of God and glory. I awoke from death in this place with no servants or riches. I am in hell."

"That is why we call him White Devil," Joseph said.

"We are going to the Great Tree," Abby said. "Can you help us?"

"If you put an end to my misery I would give you all the gold in the world," he said. "I remember gazing upon the tree in this valley, a beautiful sight, like the shores of heaven. I was dying of fever. I collapsed at the spring by the tree and quenched my thirst. Two figures of stone lay in the spring. One was a boy and the other a dog at heal. I died while drinking from that pool. I awoke under a pile of stones. My men had abandoned me thinking I was dead and my soul with God in heaven. Instead, I am cursed."

"Stop rambling White Devil," Joseph said. "Help these children."

"The secret is in the Great Tree, in that pool of eternal water," the Spaniard said. "It brings to mind a legend of a tree, a spring, and a Golden Bough—a magical bough that will protect a person from death in the underworld."

"A what?" Philip said.

"A bough, a branch, a symbol of protection. The one who bears it can come to no harm in the underworld. Hold it forth in confidence for you are chosen and will be protected." the Spaniard said.

"What underworld?" Sam asked.

"The underworld," he answered. "Where no one living can go, and the dead are lost forever. No one living is said to be able to return. You are going there, are you not?" His neck cracked loudly as he attempted to laugh. "You will find the Golden Bough at the top of the tree, I am sure of it. But whoever enters the underworld and expects to return will have to sacrifice something according to the legend. Isn't that the way it always is? Give, and take."

"Sure," Sam said. "Whatever you say."

"Thanks for the story," Abby said. "We have to hurry because we don't want to be here forever."

"You will be lucky to get home, little ones," the Spaniard said slyly. "Look at me. I am home." His neck cracked again as a sharp laugh escaped.

"Enough, White Devil," Joseph said. "It was a whim that I thought he could help. I am sorry if he gave you a fright."

"It's okay," Abby said. "We are all in this together."

"That's a fair judgment," Joseph said.

"Sad, sad, sad," the Spaniard said. "You will stay here with me when you are done. It is the nature of this place."

"No more from you White Devil," Joseph said. He kicked snow on the ancient cadaverous crank. They joined him, kicking up a torrent of snow until the conquistador was again covered in snow. The muffled voice of the Spaniard was heard one last time. "Good luck!"

***

31

After a hike, Joseph halted at a wild section of the Scenic Loop Pond. It was frozen and white with snow. It looked like a ribbon of silver poured into a fracture in the land.

"I will not go further," Joseph said. "It is too dangerous for me and my family; I don't belong beyond this water, frozen or otherwise. It is too dangerous for you as well. I would try to talk you out of your plans, but I know you must do what is right."

Abby gave Joseph a hug; Philip and Sam shook his strong hand. Philip tested the frozen pond with his foot, but Sam couldn't wait and walked out onto the ice. Luckily, it held so they made their way across the white expanse to the other side.

Once on the other side, they looked back to wave goodbye, but Joseph had already headed home to his family.

The moon was bright and full. The stars twinkled brilliantly in the clear night sky in the cold moonlit dreamscape.

They found one of the walkways that wound around and criss-crossed the zoo. They followed the snowy way to a larger avenue. Buildings were few at first, and then there were more as they neared the center of the zoo. They did not recognize anything.

Along the way they noticed lumps in the snow, some small, some big. They wove around the mounds of snow not paying them much attention.

Lights came from a building they did not recognize. It was a big building with many windows too dirty to see through. They crept up to the front door of the building to investigate. They heard music.

Turning the handle of the door ever so slightly, they pushed it inward and peaked inside. Dark tanks of water lined the wall leading right and left. The music came from the right so they crept along letting the door close behind them. The smell in the air was dank and fishy like stagnant pond water. On the floor was a faded thin carpet, moldy and stained.

They found a room of windows with a towering ceiling. A giant fish tank covered an entire wall; behind its glass was dark, murky water with ghostly shapes lurking in its depths.

Candles lit the room, burning in a derelict fountain at the center of the room. A silver, tinsel and gaudy, fake Christmas tree reflected the candlelight. Next to the silvery tree were three people who meant a lot to Philip, Sam, and Abby.

Haji Abdu played the fiddle for Betty Goody and Chang Tzu. He sang a song that recalled Christmas's past. Philip, Sam, and Abby clapped their hands when the tune ended. Their three undead friends nearly jumped out of their skins at the sound.

"As I live and breathe," Betty said as she ran up to the children and gave them each a tremendous hug. "What a night, what a gift to be with friends!"

"What are you three doing here?" Haji Abdu asked. "You should be safe at home thinking of Christmas morning and stockings full of treats."

"The town has been overrun by zombie Christmas trees," Abby said. "We are going to the Great Tree so we can save our parents and everyone in town."

"And ya'll too," Philip said. "We're going to save you too."

"So the time has come," Chang Tzu said. "The ending of all endings." He stood up from his contemplative pose. "I am ready. Are you ready?" He looked directly at Betty and Haji Abdu.

"Not entirely," Haji Abdu said.

"I have to help," Betty said. "Never abandon a friend in need."

"Let us sit for a moment before our final quest," Chang Tzu said.

They all gathered around the water fountain, lit by the candles, and spoke of all that had happened in the months that passed since their last goodbye. After all was told, they all were one, determined to do what they could.

Sam walked over to the massive aquarium, the largest he had ever seen. It was as big and deep as any room. He pressed his face against the glass trying to see into the brackish water. Something hit the glass with a watery thud. Thud, thud, thud. The noise filled the room. Dead fish, all shapes and sizes swam into the glass intent on getting at Sam. The glass seemed sure to break, but it was too thick.

"The animals have discovered your presence," Chang Tzu said. "The cold and snow has made them dormant and they see nothing. But they have noticed you three. The zoo is waking up. We have to act fast."

Haji Abdu took Betty's hand. "None of us will be left behind."

Chang Tzu led them past the murky tanks lining the wall and out the front entrance into the cold, moon-bright night. They walked briskly along the avenue.

The mounds of snow stirred as they passed. The moonlight cast shadows as furry heads poked out through the snow, aware of the living, breathing children.

Abby stopped in her tracks, Philip and Sam bumped into her. "Wait," she said to everyone. "How do we get into the Great Tree?"

"Last time, we followed Thomas through a cave," she said. "We need to figure out what to do."

Chang Tzu walked back to Abby. "There is always another way to go about doing things. A question arises and an answer follows. Because you solved a problem one way does not mean it is the correct way another time." He sat down on a mound of snow, ignoring the zombie animal stirring inside of it, and looked at the children. "How should we get to the great heights?"

"We could fly," Sam said.

"No, you have no feathers," Chang Tzu said.

"We could float," Philip said.

"No, you are not a boat or a balloon," he said.

"We climb," Abby said.

"Yes, you are kin to a monkey, accept your nature." he said.

"Enough," Haji Abdu said. "You are wasting time."

Chang Tzu shrugged and stood up, "We will climb like monkeys."

The Great Tree loomed over the zoo. It seemed to reach out and mingle with the stars in the sky. A tiny light flickered at the top of the tree. Maybe the legend of the Golden Bough was true. They had to get to that light. It was the answer.

Footsteps crunched in the snow all around them. Little paws, big paws, and stumbling, dragging paws. The animals of the zoo had followed them to the Great Tree. Dark, slow shapes came toward them. Cold death drawn to warm life.

"We cannot stop them," Haji Abdu said. Fear was in his voice. "We can escape and try again later."

"It will be too late," Chang Tzu said. "This is our only chance."

A thumping, fast whirring sound, zipped down to them from far above in the tree. A ladder of woven vine unfurled out of the darkness.

Chang Tzu grabbed the ladder. "It seems there is another. We must protect the children. We have had our say in the world, now it is time to do for others more than ourselves."

"Up you go," Haji Abdu said. Sam climbed the ladder as it creaked and swung under his weight. Abby followed and then Philip. Abby looked down at their three friends below.

"Aren't you coming too?" she asked greatly concerned.

"It's okay, dear," Betty said. "Be safe."

The zombie zoo animals approached through the snow. Bloodthirsty peacocks, an anteater, a determined porcupine, giraffes, antelopes, buffalos, even a pack of prairie dogs, and sadly the elephants Jumbo and Penny all intent on destroying them. Betty and Chang Tzu and Haji Abdu ran from the tree and away from the zombie animals.

Philip, Sam, and Abby climbed hand and foot up the vine ladder. The ladder ended at a giant limb high up the tree. Below, in the snow, it looked like all the zombie animals in the zoo had gathered and now waited, looking up at them in the tree.

High as they were above the zoo, they were still not at the top of the tree. The view was magical. Everything was covered in a blanket of snow, bright in the moonlight, cold and not a whisper of a breeze.

"Who let the ladder down?" Sam asked.

"Look at the footprints," Abby said. Small, careful footprints led further into the tangle of limbs. It was a path.

"That's the way to go," Philip said.

The footsteps in the snow led over limbs and under limbs, climbing ever upward.

Eventually, they saw a light ahead. In a great hollow in the tree, a small Indian boy sat cross-legged by a thoughtful fire on a flat stone. In the hollow, they could see an impressive collection of odds and ends.

"Finally," the boy said. His voice was formal and merry. He had dark eyes, straight, dark hair that came to his shoulders, and well worn buckskins. He was dead, just like the others. When he stood up, he was shorter than Abby and younger.

"You took too long to climb the ladder," he said. "I wanted to have a brighter fire to welcome you. Come sit in a circle around the fire."

When they settled, the boy looked at each of them in turn. The glow of the fire lit their features and closed out the rest of the world. The warmth of the fire made them feel much better.

"I am Ogue. I saw you during the summer and I hoped to meet you," he said. "I knew you would return."

Before they could say anything, Ogue began, "Within this sacred circle, protected by the fire given to us by Grandmother Spider, we wish to fulfill the right way." He tied a red strip of cloth around his forehead. He gave them each a piece of cloth, and they tied them tightly, as well. Together they looked like a tribe.

Ogue brought forth a long smoking pipe with a red stone bowl carved in the shape of a squirrel. He picked a glowing twig from the fire and placed the bright end to the hollow in the back of the squirrel and puffed until smoke rose. He passed the pipe to Philip. He took a draw and coughed. He passed it to Sam, but he was tough and didn't cough. Abby took the pipe, smoked bravely and passed it back to Ogue. He placed the pipe at his side and looked deep into the fire and thought about what he must say. The smoke made them feel light-headed and dreamy.

The moon was full and bright above them, the stars countless, the Dog Star, brightest of all, tailed the moon. The Great Tree mingled with the heavens.

"A long time ago, when time meant something to me, I lost my dog. I looked and looked for her. Days passed, but I could not let that dog go. On the fourth day, I was so tired I could not make it home. I made a small fire next to this tree. I was so worried about my dog. I made a figure of myself and my dog out of clay and baked them in the fire. When they were hardened I tossed them in the spring so that fate would bring us together. A little fish in the pool circled my offerings and guarded them. I was hungry and tired, but I could not make myself catch that fish and eat it. Instead, in my weakness, I lay down against the tree and fell asleep. But I did not sleep. I died. A vision came to me and I saw clearly. My dog was at the spring. She took a drink and with a yelp of surprise she vanished into the pool. Ever since, I have lived in the Great Tree, not daring to touch the spring for the underworld that is below. My poor dog has to endure it. It is a burden."

"Your dog fell in the spring," Abby said dreamily.

"No," Ogue said. "She was pulled in against her will to live with Uktena for all eternity."

"That's a shame," Sam said staring at the fire for a moment and then he lay back against the tree and looked up at the stars.

"What is Uktena?" Philip asked.

"Uktena lives in the underworld and plays tricks on the living. There is no reason to Uktena." Ogue said.

Philip let it go. It sounded like a fairy tale or myth to him.

Abby thought for a long time, "I threw a little figurine into the spring and made that jerk Thomas disappear forever."

"I know," Ogue said. 'I watched it all happen from the top of the tree.'

"I also have brought with me a little statue of a dog that a strange old man once took from this spring when he was a boy," Abby said. She couldn't quite get her thoughts together.

Ogue jumped up. A gorget of white shell with a thunderbird etched in black lines hung from his neck. "Let me see," he almost shouted.

Abby tried to get it out of her pocket, but it was stuck. She lay back on her back and kept digging. She brought forth the worn, tan colored figure of a dog sitting on its haunches and held it to the light of the fire. "Ta da," she exclaimed.

Ogue reached for it, but Abby wouldn't let him have it. "If you take this what will you do?" she asked him.

"I will put it back in the spring and wish for my dog to return, and then everything will be back the way it should be," he said.

"What is the way things should be?" Sam asked. "Look around. Everyone here is a zombie. We don't want any more zombies. No more zombies!"

"Yeah, things can't stay the same," Philip said. "We have to change things."

"You are right," Ogue said. "You keep the figurine. We will go to the spring and see what happens."

"Do you know of a Golden Bough?" Abby asked.

"Yes," he said. "High in the tree, there is a branch that is green all year, which turns gold in winter. But always it turns green in spring. It never dies."

"Show us and we will get your dog back," she said.

Ogue looked deep into the fire. "I have seen a thousand years pass. People arrive and change things and then they leave. I have watched and learned from others, but none have wanted to learn from me."

Ogue stood up, "I will show you the Golden Bough. Get up while there is time. Midnight is close and the moon is high—a magic time! If we are quick, we can save us all!"

One by one, they followed Ogue up the tree. Higher and higher, where the Great Tree was thin and the branches were craggy. They had to watch their step.

Just shy of the very tip-top of the tree, a cluster of golden delicate leaves and pearly berries clung to the highest branch. The Golden Bough was just a growth of mistletoe the size of a cooking pot—not too big, not too small.

"That's it?" Sam said. "What do we do with it?"

"Whoever takes a twig from the Golden Bough will be protected from harm," Ogue said. "As long as it never touches the ground."

"You mean you can't be hurt?" Philip asked.

"You can't be harmed," Ogue said. "But only in the underworld."

Abby pinched a twig of the golden leaves and pearly berries from the Golden Bough and wrapped a piece of string around the end. She hung it around her neck.

Ogue looked surprised.

"It's done. What do we do now?" Abby said.

"We climb down."

***

32

Ogue showed them a place to crawl down through the tree. They found themselves on the inside looking down at the peaceful spring far below. There were the boulders they had stood on, the grassy lawn around the clear pool, and the spiral of stones winding from the center to the outer edge of the water. That terrible night during the summer came back to their minds and how they had narrowly escaped with their lives. Thomas Meanwell was long gone. But the memory of when he became a zombie and attacked them was still alive.

They climbed down, weaving in and out of the inside of the Great Tree and closer to the spring.

As Ogue climbed, he mis-stepped and dangled from a branch by one hand. Abby tried to help him, but he lost his grip and grabbed Abby by her jean pocket which ripped away at the stitches. The figurine of the dog dropped out and fell into the darkness below followed by Ogue.

Ogue fell fast and far and landed with a thud on the ground below. They could see him in the shadows cast by the moonlight shining brightly above. The figurine landed in the spring with splash.

"No!" Abby yelled. Philip and Sam looked shocked.

Ogue sat up, "I'm alright."

Just then the moon shown brilliantly on the spring pool hidden in the Great Tree—a perfect alignment. Everything inside the tree took on a silvery glow.

The spiral of stones shown clearly and appeared to lead down farther than one could see. The water was no longer water. Now there was only clear nothingness. Nothing reflected from its surface and now only a spiral path could be seen. The colorful fish that guarded the spring was gone. The figurine of the boy and the dog were gone as well.

They hurried down to meet Ogue. At the edge of the spring that was no longer a spring they peered with amazement at the spiral that went far down into the unknown. No edges and no boundaries could be discerned.

Ogue looked up at the moon, "The time to go is now," he said. "The moon has opened the spring."

Abby pulled the sprig of the Golden Bough from around her neck and gripped it tightly in her right hand. She held out her left hand, "Who's going with me?" she asked.

Ogue, Philip, and Sam stepped forward to grab her hand. Before any of them could react, something seemed to grab her foot and dragged her into the spring.

The boys yelled in utter fear for Abby. But they were also afraid to go near the spring because they were not protected by the Golden Bough. Only Abby was protected.

Abby felt herself fall into a void and land on the hard gravel of the spiral in the spring. A path stretched endlessly before her. Above, she could see the opening of the spring and Philip, Sam, and Ogue looking down at her. They could not see her.

From above, the spiral path had looked narrow, but once Abby started walking, she found that it quickly widened. Soon all she saw was the pebble strewn path and nothing else. She walked and walked, and nothing seemed to matter except to keep on walking.

She held the sprig of mistletoe high to see the way. It glowed golden and furious in her hand. She wasn't scared. Instead, she felt brave when she thought of her parents trapped in the house and of her brothers and friends and the animals in the zoo. She touched the strip of cloth that Ogue had given her, still tied around her head, red and bold.

Suddenly, she stopped. She thought she heard something.

She continued walking. There it was again!

She turned around to see if someone was behind her. In the luminous glow of the golden mistletoe, was a brute of a dog, red-wheat in color, dark snout, bone-thin, and with bright eager eyes. It looked up at her with a questioning gaze. It was ready to play or go where the action was.

Abby had been ready to scream. Now she laughed and knelt down to pet the friendly dog. The dog was eager for attention and licked her face. It sat down and looked at her, reminding her of the figurine of the dog. "Are you lost?" she asked. The cadaverous dog wagged its tail and seemed to smile.

A trusting face looked up at her, "Do you want to go home?" she asked. Gravel scattered with each furious sweep of its tail. It jumped up with a terrible cracking of joints and ran off down the path. "No, that's the wrong way!" she yelled. "Come on, you silly dog, follow me home!"

She ran after the dog, gravel crunching under foot and holding the glowing sprig of mistletoe in front of her. The dog waited for her where the path ended at a deep pool of water that stretched in all directions into the darkness. The gravel beneath her feet had turned to sand and the path forward was obscured. The dog waited no longer, turned, and walked into the water expecting her to follow. It looked like water, but Abby wasn't sure. It didn't ripple when the dog disappeared into it.

"Dog!" she called. "Come back!"

Abby didn't know what to do. She looked around, holding the sprig up to see. Behind her the gravel path seemed far away. It spiraled up to a pinhole in the darkness far above. She felt panicky, so she sat down in the soft sand and put her face in her hands. "What do I do?" she said on the verge of crying desperately.

Shoosh-ta, shoosh-ta. She heard a rattle and a stomp. They grew louder and rhythmic. She brought her head up from her hands and looked around. The sound stopped. At the edge of the sand near the water, four piles of sticks lay a few paces apart. She could see footprints form in the sand. No one was there. She jumped up not knowing what was going on. She put her hands to her face again, trying to keep the panic away. With her eyes closed, she heard the rhythmic stomp and rattle, and saw the figure dancing around the piles of sticks. She uncovered her face and the sound and the figure were gone.

She wanted to run but there was nowhere to go. She decided to be brave. She pulled the red headband over her eyes so she wouldn't be tempted to open her eyes again and she looked hard at the figure in front of her dancing steadily around in a circle. The dancer was the strangest person, if it was a person, she had ever seen. Much taller than a man, and made, it seemed, of pine needles, bleached white animal bones, leaves, and cobwebs, held together with vines. The bones didn't belong together—small and large and in the wrong place, from rodents, deer, birds, reptiles and toads, and insects, tumbling around and making no sense. Instead of a face, there was the bleached white skull of a deer with antlers worn and brittle, too long weathered in the sun and rain. Blue and red patterns swirled across that visage, the meaning lost to Abby.

The rattle came from turtle shell rattles strapped to the dancer's legs. Each stomp brought the sound.

Abby should be terrified but there was nothing to be afraid of. She felt no animosity directed toward her. What she wanted to do most was join the dance.

Eyes still covered by the red cloth, she went behind the figure and fell in line, mimicking the steps. She stomped in time with the figure and felt the power.

As they danced in a circle, the water drained away inch by inch, and the shoreline receded until there was no water left. They had made the water go away and now they were surrounded by an expanse of wet sand, and curiously, the continuing path. The dog's footprints, pressed in the sand, led on.

The dancing figure stopped and turned to Abby. The bluest blue and the reddest red swirled, forming intricate patterns within the bleached bone and detritus where a face should be. Abby did not think this was a man or a woman. She thought of what Ogue had told them.

"Are you Uktena?" she asked. The strange figure bowed low to her. "Are you a person?" she asked. Uktena shook its antlered head. "Are you a spirit?" she asked. Uktena clapped its twig and bone hands together. Abby assumed this meant she had guessed close enough to the truth.

A thought tumbled out that had been bothering Abby for some time.

"Did a man named Thomas Meanwell come down here a few months ago?" she asked. Uktena bent down and gazed at her face for a moment. Then it stretched to its full height, looked upward, and spread its arms wide. It made a spiral gesture with its hand and pointed up.

Abby looked up with her eyes still covered with the red cloth. She could see stars above, stars all around, even stars below her feet when she looked closely enough.

The longer she looked the clearer the stars, as well as the moon above, became. She noticed a faint glow around them. An electric, filamentary, swirling rotated on the periphery like a funnel that led out into space and far beyond to impossible distances connecting and reaching far out to the stars. She looked down and she saw the same thing beneath her feet.

"So Thomas went up there?" she said. Uktena nodded. It reached into its torso and pulled out the figurine that Abby had thrown at Thomas and which had landed in the spring. Reached again, it pulled out the dog figurine that had fallen from her pocket into the spring. Uktena held each hardened, stone-like, clay figure in a hand outstretched toward Abby.

"What?" she said. "Do you want me to take them? Do you want me to choose one? I don't want them. They aren't mine, and they don't belong to you. Ogue made them. He didn't know this would happen. He only wanted to find his dog." Uktena watched her, the colors swirling on its grim visage. She was getting mad. "I'm going to go find that dog." She pushed the headband onto her forehead and opened her eyes. Uktena was gone.

. She walked determinedly down the sandy path following the dog tracks and determined to find Ogue's lost dog. "If you lose a dog, you better go find it," she thought to herself. She held the Golden Bough before her, the way ahead was clear. With the water gone, she walked far, farther than anyone alive had ever walked before. But she did not know this.

After what seemed an eternity, she heard the dog urgently barking ahead in the dark, so she quickened her pace. She found the dog, barking madly and leaning over a hole in the ground big enough to drive a car through. Mud was packed in heaps around the hole and a terrible smell came from it.

"C'mon dog, I'm taking you back to your master," she said. The dog barely noticed her, and continued barking.

"C'mon poochie, come here," she tried baby talk and kissing noises, to get the dog's attention. "You want to see Ogue, don't ya? I know you do. If you just come with me, we can get the heck out of here, and we can all be happy again."

The dog perked up at the name Ogue. He padded over to her, then turned and growled at the hole in the ground. A monstrous shape crawled out from the depths of the muddy hole. Pinchers the size of sofas; black, alien, orb eyes; spiny feelers testing the air—a rust-red crustacean the size of a school bus scrambled out of its lair and searched now for the intruders that awakened it.

Abby took a few steps back as silently as possible, but the dog barked at the enormous crustacean, which Abby thought looked like a giant crawdad.

Abby took off running back the way she came. The dog must have known this was good idea and fell in behind her. She ran for her life through the expanse of sand. She could hear the skittering of the crustacean's legs in the sand and the clack of its claws ready to crush her.

She found the prayer stick bundles where she and Uktena had danced and talked. "I failed. I did it all wrong. Nothing happened the way it was supposed to. I didn't save the zoo or mom and dad. I didn't get the figurines, but I did get the dog." These thoughts hammered around in her mind trying to undermine her will.

She ran until she found the spiral path leading up to the real world, which was just a tiny dot in the darkness above. The stars were gone, the electric spiral of the cosmos was gone, and she didn't want to close her eyes again.

The dog ran ahead and started up the gravely spiral, leading the way. Abby lagged behind.

The terrible crustacean followed. She ran as fast as she could but it was not fast enough. The giant crustacean was close and gaining. She stopped and turned to face the beast. She didn't want to be a victim. "If this is the way it ends, so be it!" she said to herself.

The deadly pinchers came around a turn along the spiral path and the dark eyes the size of hubcaps fixed on her. A hundred things flashed in her mind. One idea stuck. She reached into the shoulder bag still at her side and brandished the flare gun Frank had given her for emergencies. This felt like an emergency.

She pointed and pulled the trigger. The trigger wouldn't budge. She looked at the gun with the wide, short barrel and pistol grip. Then she flipped the safety switch and aimed again. This time the gun launched a fireball that made her trip backward, and she landed on her back. The red-orange shot arced out of the gun and hit explosively on the hard shell of the spiny beast. It screeched loudly, more at being blinded by the light than anything. The creature seemed to have met its match and scuttled away into the darkness and back to its home.

Abby got up and took off. She climbed higher and higher until the spiral path was only a narrow ledge, and she was not sure she could hold on. Around and around she went, until all of a sudden she poked her head out into the clearing inside the Great Tree. Philip and Sam cheered when they saw her. At long last! Her brothers overwhelmed her with hugs. The Golden Bough still gripped in her hand had withered. She wrapped it in her red headband and put it in her pocket.

"You did it! You made it back, and you found Ogue's dog!" Philip said, happy to have his sister back.

"We were afraid to go after you," Sam said.

"I'm not sure what I did," Abby said. "It doesn't feel like anything changed."

The ground shook and a thunderous rumbling started deep beneath the Great Tree. The strangest feeling came over them. Abby sensed a thought, "You may go forward." And the feeling grew.

Ogue knelt on the ground with his dog, finally after years and years, reunited with the happy tail-wagging dog. He smiled and even the dog smiled. Both were happy and together and perfect. "I can never thank you enough," Ogue said. "You three have done something noble and selfless, especially you, Abby. Don't give up on those you love, and they won't give up on you." Ogue patted his dog, and the dog lifted a paw in return. "And never give up on yourself."

The last sliver of the moon passed above the Great Tree. The spring was again just a pool of water, the spiral of stones and the fish, blue and red, swam again in the center. The underworld was closed to the living once more. It was over.

Before Abby could say anything, Ogue and his dog faded away.

"No, wait!" she yelled. But they were gone. The ground beneath rumbled again. They were alone in the cold, winter night.

"Did it work?" Philip asked. "Do you think mom and dad are okay?"

"I don't know," Abby said. She felt like crying after watching Ogue and his dog disappear.

"Do you think the animals are back to normal?" Sam wondered.

"Maybe," Abby said.

The rumbling beneath them became louder and knocked them down. The air seemed to charge and glow, and every time they shut their eyes the ground looked thin and transparent. Stars and darkness flashed beneath them.

"Keep your eyes open!" Abby yelled. "We have to climb the tree."

They climbed up the Great Tree, frantically grabbing roots and limbs. They found their way back to Ogue's den. The sacred fire he built still burned faintly. The air was charged with energy, electric, massive, radiating around them, up through the Great Tree, out into the night sky, and into space.

They threw sticks on the sacred fire and huddled around it, holding hands tightly and hoping not to be taken away. They were protected as time caught up to the undead at the zoo.

The sacred fire suddenly flamed high in front of them. Their hands were gripped tightly as if they were holding onto their lives. They were afraid to let go.

The spiral of energy reached out to the stars and connected in filaments far, far, away. The glowing energy spread out around the base of the Great Tree and drifted like smoke, further and further outward, engulfing the zoo animals that had crowded around the Great Tree, spreading into the woods and buildings of the zoo.

Like an invisible bubble expanding, the energy spread to the town and countryside, touching on all that once lived and that still lived—the undead. The energy retracted suddenly back to the Great Tree and joined the spiral filament rotating out into space.

Philip, Sam, and Abby were spared from the engine of the galaxy. They only saw the sacred fire before them.

The ground below the Great Tree quit rumbling. All they could hear was the crackling of the wood in the fire. The cold of winter seeped into the layers of their clothes. It was over, whatever it was.

"Wow!" Sam said. "Are we still alive?"

"Looks like it," Philip said.

"I want to go home," Abby said.

Philip and Sam agreed.

❊❊❊

33

The sacred fire died and the ashes grew cold on the flat rock resting in the crook high in the branches of the Great Tree. The children traced their way back to Ogue's vine ladder and climbed down the tree.

Animal tracks were everywhere in the snow but the animals were gone. It was quiet and cold.

They found the footprints of Haji Abdu, Betty, and Chang Tzu in the snow, leading deeper into the zoo. They followed hoping to find their friends.

Through the snow they trudged. Three set of footprints became two, then one. They followed the last lonely set of prints.

They came to a familiar bridge that spanned the Scenic Loop Pond that coursed through the zoo. On the bridge a figure stood silently looking out at the frozen pond.

"Hello, my friends," Haji Abdu called to them. "Come enjoy the view with me."

They joined him on the bridge. "I've always loved this view." He said. "The way the trees reflect off the water in the spring, the animals doing what animals do. I can't count how many times I have stood here. It is all so familiar to me. I don't know if I am ready to leave."

Abby took his hand. He turned and looked down at the sweet girl. His fierce eyes, forked beard, and heavy mustache would have intimidated many people, but not Abby.

"I'm sorry," she said. "I didn't want any of you to leave for good."

"You did the right thing. We have been here far too long. All things pass. If they didn't, then the world would be a terrible place with no progress." He looked at the three kids standing there in the snow with him. "I want you to do something for me. Treat the animals kindly, they have feelings too, and don't fret about us. We had our time, and now it's time to say good bye."

Haji Abdu looked out onto the fine winter night from the snow-covered bridge, beyond the shore of the pond, the trees, the buildings of the zoo, and he smiled to himself and faded away without even realizing it. There were only his footprints in the snow.

They were alone on the bridge. If fact, they were alone in the zoo.

"It's cold," Abby said.

With that they said goodbye, and started back toward the way they had entered the zoo.

They were silent as they trudged through the snow. As they walked, they felt the energy that held the zoo together dissipate. The buildings weakened, a brick tumbled here and there, a wall collapsed, and a roof came down. There was a crash of window glass in the distance. Time was catching up at the zoo.

They walked past Joseph and Fannie Cobb's cabin. The roof had sunk, the walls leaned inward, and the chimney threatened to collapse.

They followed their steps back to the gate at the back of the zoo. As they squeezed through, the gate fell outward with into the snow. No need to keep it closed anymore. They were finished with the Forest Heights Zoological Park.

They ran to the Quonset hut to find Frank. The lights were still on when they arrived. They ran past the big duck and warmed up at the pot belly stove.

They heard something crash in the building. A moment later, Frank stumbled up and sat down in his brother's chair.

"Frank, how are you still alive?" Abby said.

"Sheer will power," Frank said managing a smile. "I'm glad to see you. Ya'll have been the best friends I have known in a long time—maybe, ever. I'll never forget."

Frank remembered something. "Make sure Stan gets home from the hospital. Ya'll are good kids." And then he disappeared forever.

"Oh no, Frank," Abby said, brushing away tears.

"Is everybody gone?" Sam said.

"Let's go home," Philip said.

As they left the building, they flipped the light switch off and closed the doors. The fire in the stove would burn itself out.

They left the Quonset hut and walked to the main road. The town was silent and seemed big and unfamiliar. They struggled up the last street, slipping and sliding, trying to find a foothold in the white blanket of snow. Around the last corner they saw their house.

They burst into the kitchen. The house was silent. Philip led the way through the house and down the hall to their parent's room.

The Christmas tree was lying on the floor in the hallway. The mass of tentacle roots that had filled the hallway and barred the bedroom door were gone. The tree looked as normal as can be.

Philip opened the door to their parent's bedroom. Mr. and Mrs. Pruitt were asleep on the bed. The television was on.

"Mom, dad," Sam said. "We're back. Everything's okay. The Christmas tree is back to normal. We saved you."

Mrs. Pruitt mumbled and turned over on her side. Mr. Pruitt got up and turned the television off, and then lay back down sinking deeper into his pillow. Neither of them woke. Philip, Sam, and Abby looked at each other confused. Philip closed the door and let their parents sleep.

Philip and Sam hauled the Christmas tree back into the living room. Abby helped them set it upright and replaced the scattered decorations. A few branches were bent in funny directions, but for the most part it looked as cheery and festive as it did at the beginning of the evening.

Philip lay on the couch, Sam curled up in a chair, and, still wearing her coat, Abby lay down behind the Christmas tree.

Before Abby fell asleep, she felt something in her pocket. She touched something cold and gasped. In her hand she held the two fired-clay figurines, a boy and a dog, worn with age. How they got in her pocket she would never know. Later, she would keep them on a shelf in her room to remind her of their adventure, along with the zoo book and a framed picture that Betty must have stuck in her bag. The picture was of grandpa with Betty and Warren sitting in a small carriage harnessed to a grouchy looking ostrich. She fell asleep under the warm, twinkling lights of the Christmas tree.

It was well into morning when they woke to the sounds and smells of coffee brewing and the clanking of dishes in the kitchen. Usually on Christmas morning they would have been up at the crack of dawn, but today they had a good reason to sleep late.

It only took a moment to remember that it was the morning of the most important day of the year, Christmas Day. Under the tree were piles of presents all carefully wrapped, the stockings were stuffed full, and they smelled candy and chocolate and peppermint.

They were up in a flash. Moving on.

THE END

❈❈❈